rn or renew by
⌐ 'ow

Books by Brian Moore

The Lonely Passion of Judith Hearne
The Feast of Lupercal
The Luck of Ginger Coffey
An Answer from Limbo
Canada (*with the editors of* Life)
The Emperor of Ice-Cream
I Am Mary Dunne
Fergus
The Revolution Script
Catholics
The Great Victorian Collection
The Doctor's Wife
The Mangan Inheritance
The Temptation of Eileen Hughes

The Temptation of Eileen Hughes

The

Temptation of

Eileen Hughes

Brian Moore

McClelland and Stewart

Copyright © 1981 by Brian Moore
All rights reserved
Designed by Cynthia Krupat
ISBN 0-7710-6419-5
The Canadian Publishers
McClelland and Stewart Limited
25 Hollinger Road, Toronto M4B 3G2
Printed in the United States of America

For Jean

The Temptation of Eileen Hughes

Monday, August 25

"What do you mean there's no room for her?" Bernard said. "Didn't you get my letter?"

The Assistant Manager went to a cabinet and took out a file, turning sheets of paper until he found the letter. Eileen could tell he was wary of Bernard.

"Is that it?" Bernard said. "Well, you'll see that I asked for a single room for Miss Hughes on the Garden Court side, near our suite, if possible."

The Assistant Manager consulted the letter. "So you did. Indeed, you did. I'm most terribly sorry. It's just that we're so used to booking you and Mrs. McAuley into your regular suite that we didn't notice this extra request. It's our fault, completely."

"Well, then," Bernard said, and waited.

But the Assistant Manager seemed flustered. "I'm afraid we're completely booked. I'll ring around to some other hotels at once. It won't be easy, though. London is full of visitors this week."

"We don't want her staying in another hotel," Bernard said in a very sharp voice.

"Then may I make a suggestion?" the Assistant Manager said. "We could put a foldaway bed in the sitting room of your suite. The young lady could sleep there, and in the daytime we'd take the bed out so that you'd have the use of the room."

Which would be all right, Eileen thought, but saw that Bernard was looking at Mona as if waiting for Mona to decide. And when Mona said nothing, Bernard told the Assistant Manager, "I'm sorry, but I don't think that would suit us."

"Well, I do have one other suggestion, in that case," the Assistant Manager said. "We have a few rooms on the top floor, maid's rooms they were, in the days when some of our guests traveled with their own ladies' maids. But they're not very comfortable, I warn you."

"Maid's rooms." Bernard made a face.

"Yes, well, it was just a thought. As we have nothing else."

"I'm sure it would be all right," Eileen said.

"Then why not take a look at it," Mona said. "Bernard, you go with her." She turned to the Assistant Manager. "I think I'll go up to our suite now."

"Certainly, Mrs. McAuley." The Assistant Manager signaled for a porter. "This way, please." And then they all got in the lift together, Mona and Bernard and Eileen and the Assistant Manager and the porter. The Assistant Manager was young and good-looking and had a very nice smile. He smiled apologetically at Eileen as he bumped into her when the lift stopped at the seventh floor to let Mona and the porter out. "Sorry," he said, and she said that was quite all right. When they reached the top floor he told them: "This way, please," and led them into a corridor, past a door marked LAUNDRY HAMPERS and one marked SERVICE/KEEP OUT. Halfway down the corridor he unlocked a door into a tiny room with a low ceiling, a narrow single bed, and an old wardrobe. There was a skylight window and a small sink. Eileen went in. Things were not starting out as she had hoped.

"Oh, oh," said Bernard's voice behind her.

"No, this is lovely," she said quickly.

"Are you sure?"

"Yes, this will do, all right."

"Well, in that case shall I have your luggage sent up?" the Assistant Manager asked.

She said yes, thanks, and smiled at him as he gave her the room key. "I'm sorry about the mixup," he told Bernard. "Very sorry." And then, to her, "I hope you enjoy your stay with us, Miss Hughes."

She said she was sure she would. When the Assistant Manager went out, Bernard sat on the little bed, then bounced up and down. "Hard as rocks."

"I like a hard bed," she said. She wished he wouldn't bounce like that on the bed she would be sleeping in.

"A maid's room. And here we were planning to treat you like royalty," he said, in his jokey way. "Seriously, it's like a board, this bed. Try it. Just try it."

"Talking about royalty—" she said. She did not want to sit on the bed with him. "Is it really true we're right beside Buckingham Palace?"

He got up and went to the dirty skylight window. He looked out and said, "Come here."

All she could see were slate rooftops, gray sky, rain, rain.

"See that wall over there, the one with the iron spikes on top?"

She said she did.

"That's the wall of Buckingham Palace. We'll go around there later. Now, here's the plan. We'll rest for an hour, have a wash and so on. Mona likes a rest when

she gets off a plane. Then you can meet us in our suite
for coffee, and after that I have a car ordered to take
us sightseeing. How does that strike you?"

"Lovely."

"I'm raging about the room, though. Stupid bloody
people not reading my letter. I should have telephoned
to check up."

"Oh, no, it's grand, really it is."

"All right, then. See you in a little while."

He went out and she heard him speaking to someone
in the corridor, and then someone knocked on her
door and it was a porter who brought in her suitcase.
When she went to her purse for a tip, the porter said
the gentleman had already taken care of it. She could
unpack, she supposed, but instead went to the window
and looked out at the wall he said was Buckingham
Palace. Bernard and Mona would be resting in their
suite. A whole hour she'd be sitting in this wee room,
waiting for them. She had a notion to slip out now and
have a quick look at the palace. She felt dishonest about
it, it was like slipping out of the shop when you were
supposed to be working, but anyway, she locked the
room door and went down to the lobby. When she got
out of the lift on the ground floor, she was right beside
a desk where there were two young hall porters, boys
her own age, wearing livery coats with silver buttons.
She went up to the desk. They were doing something
and didn't look up for a minute, but when they did
she gave them a smile. One was short and the other
was tall and good-looking. "Help you, miss?" the short
one asked.

"Yes, well, I just wondered if you could tell me the
quickest way to Buckingham Palace?"

"Buckingham Palace," the tall one said. He pointed
to a big map under glass on the desk top in front of him.

"Right around the corner, see? We're here. First left, then left again, and you'll be slap up against it."

"First left, and left again?"

"Right. Come along, I'll start you off." The tall one came from behind the desk and went with her out the front door of the hotel and stood beside her on the steps as he pointed out the way. "Just keep bearing left."

"Oh, thanks. Thanks very much. That's very nice of you. It's my first time in London," she said, and then caught herself. Maybe as usual she had said too much. What does he care if it's my first time here? But he smiled back.

"Have a nice walk, then," he said.

As she went down the steps, suddenly she felt happy. Maybe English boys were different. Maybe it wasn't her fault with the boys at home, maybe it was their fault, always backing off if she tried to be friendly, or being too friendly themselves, trying to get a feel of her breasts. Maybe the boys were nicer here. Or more easily pleased. And now, as she began to walk, she met up with a great mob of people who were coming up the street from what looked like a big railway station, women in headscarves, men in hats carrying rolled umbrellas and briefcases. Englishmen. She looked right at them, wondering if they *were* different from the men at home, but met familiar male stares, eyes which moved from her legs up to her face, assessing her. On she went toward Buckingham Palace, passing a gate painted black and gold that had a sign on it saying it was the *Royal Mews* and then, a bit farther on, another that said the *Queen's Gallery*. She bore left as the tall porter had told her to until she came out in front of a huge building in white stone like Belfast City Hall, but far bigger; in front of it was a red stone courtyard with high iron railings, a rotunda, and a great mall leading to a big avenue with

[7]

other avenues going off to each side. Soldiers in black busby hats and red tunics, stock-still in sentry boxes, and the real guards, policemen in twos and threes, at each gate. A squall of wind swept suddenly across the palace yard and she turned her head away, avoiding the gust. I am here. And because I've seen this, maybe I'll see all those other places too, New York and Paris, and someday maybe I'll even live someplace like this with a job that will pay me enough to send plenty of money home to Mama.

She looked up at the great windows above the palace courtyard. The Queen is in there, maybe sitting with her corgis or getting ready to go out to some big do. She thought of the Queen's face, a disapproving face, a face that intimidated her. Under the Queen's windows a busbied soldier stepped out of his sentry box, came to attention with a crash of booted heels, shouldered his rifle, and went stiffleg stride along the palace wall. Clustered around the palace railings, tourists focused their cameras, posing for each other to record their presence on this scene. She turned and walked a few paces away from the people at the railings, imagining as she often did that she was someone else. Now she was a London girl with a good office job, or maybe a nurse who had come here to Buckingham Palace because it was a handy place to meet her boy friend. She stood, looking up at the sweep of the Victoria Memorial, at the cars and taxis whizzing around it and going off up the royal avenues. She was tall and thin and wore her dark hair long, brushed straight, falling to her shoulders. Her skin was statue white, her eyes a clear light blue. She was a girl some men might find beautiful, but so far she had no suspicion of that. Men, boys, had always made her nervous. She wanted to be friendly, wanted them to like her, but somehow she seemed to say too little, or smile too much. And sometimes she couldn't think of a thing to say to them. She lived with her mother. Today was the first time, except for her visit to Dublin with the McAuleys earlier this year, that she had ever been really away on her own. Of course, being with the McAuleys was not the same as being on your own. Still, here she was in London, her first time across the water. And, of course, without the McAuleys she could never have afforded it.

Now, as she stood looking up at the statuary in the Victoria Memorial, a clock struck behind her, somewhere in the city. She tried to count: she had no watch. Was that the half hour, half-ten? Or later? What if Bernard McAuley had had enough rest and decided to go up to her room to see if she was ready. She turned back, hurrying past the palace railings and the soldiers in their sentry boxes, past the Queen's Gallery and the Royal Mews. What would the McAuleys say to each other if they found out she had left the hotel without telling them? They seemed in bad form already, they had hardly spoken a word to each other on the way to Belfast airport or on the flight to London. It would be terrible to annoy them now at the beginning of the holiday they were paying for her. She had been silly to come out like this and risk being caught.

But when she got to the hotel there was no sign of them, at least not in the lobby. As she pressed the button for the lift, the young porters saw her and she smiled at them. "Thank you," she called out to them. "I found it all right."

"See Prince Charles, by any chance?"

"Oh, no," she said. She laughed to show them she knew it was a joke, to be friendly toward them, but the tall one had picked up the phone and the short one was beginning to answer some guest's question. They were probably jokey like that with everybody, it was probably a way of getting tips. The lift came. She glanced back at them as she got in, ready to wave or smile if they looked up. But they were busy.

Mona McAuley was lying on the bed when she heard her husband come out of the bathroom. She at once shut her eyes, pretending sleep. For the past two days she had not said one pleasant word to him, and no wonder, the way he had tried to trick her and suddenly spring Eileen on her at the last minute, when he had the tickets bought, the London arrangements all made, and the girl with her suitcase packed. In fact, he might have managed to do just that had she not gone into the shop on Friday to be confronted with Eileen asking what she should wear on the plane. Oh, he had gone right around the bend, there was no doubt about it. Rage filled her when she thought of all she had done to accommodate him lately. This was her thanks, on the one holiday that was supposed to be for *her*. She heard him cross the bedroom and slip into the sitting room of the suite, heard him close the door quietly so as not to disturb her, then whisper on the phone, getting room service to send up coffee and croissants and roses that he had ordered specially. She knew him and his surprise treats.

She lay for a few minutes until she heard the waiter come in with the coffee. She got up then. One thing he had taught her was to be on time. She had been a pharmacist before her marriage, working at Crowley's in Lismore, and the last thing she had wanted to do was to go on working. But six months later she was bored stiff, sitting in her grand new house with a full-time housekeeper and a maid and not a hand's turn to do. That was when Bernard suddenly promised to show her the ropes in the big shop in Royal Street. I want somebody to take my place there on a day-to-day basis, he said. She thought he was joking, how could she run McAuleys? But he said there are only two things you have to do. Always be on time, and if you promise to do something, be sure you do it. And had taken time off from his other businesses to go in with her every morning and show her how to buy stock and deal with travelers and keep an eye on the department heads and order for special times like Christmas and schools opening. He let her make decisions on her own, decisions that involved thousands of pounds. Of course she had wondered at the time if it was because he had suddenly stopped being so attentive in other ways. About that time she realized he must be masturbating on the couch up in his study. He kept dirty books up there and pictures of women, and besides, she saw the signs of it. Maybe he let her run the shop just to keep her quiet. Still, he had taught her a lot about the business. When you promise to do something, be sure you do it. Well, that was what he hadn't done this week.

She put on her face and dressed herself in a tweed skirt and blouse, then a blazer, and to finish it off she tied a Hermès scarf around the handle of her handbag. When the little clock on the night table said eleven exactly, she opened the bedroom door and went into the sitting room. She saw that he had changed from the jeans he had worn on the plane to a gray pinstripe suit. He had all his suits made by an expensive London tailor. He made fun of himself for it, joking about a mick from Lismore getting himself up like English gentry. She knew he made that sort of remark partly to forestall other people saying it about him, but she also knew it wasn't that simple. He liked things to be perfect. He had always had money and knew how to use it to make his life comfortable. Still, that was only part of it. She would never understand him. Who could? His mocking him-self had another side to it. It wasn't just to protect himself from ridicule. It was, she sometimes thought, as though he felt he was an imposter in his own life.

"Did you call Eileen?" she asked, and added, "Need I ask?"

"Yes, I just sent up for her." He was still trying to play the diplomat. "Oh, by the way," he said, "here's our schedule." He held out a Xerox sheet as though she were a dog that might bite him. "Maybe you'd take a look at it and tell me if it's all right?"

She put the sheet close to her eyes. It was an annoyance to her that her eyes would not tolerate contact lenses. He had put down time and place for everything: restaurants, museums, theaters. "Do you have bookings for all these things?"

"Yes, but you don't have to come to something if you don't want to. I can always say you're visiting that school friend of yours."

"Three tickets for theaters," Mona said. "That's a shocking waste."

"Ah, but surely you'll come to *some* of them."

"I told you, no."

He was going to say something, but she silenced him. "Somebody at the door."

He turned. There was a second uncertain knock. "Guess who?" she said.

He went at once. She watched him, transformed at sight of the girl, leading her to the table, secretly proud of the special roses he had ordered. She could imagine him coming home before lunch some weekday last spring, the big Mercedes crunching up the gravel driveway of Tullymore, see him getting out and going in through the greenhouse, taking off the rubber boots he wore when he went out to his construction sites, then telling Mrs. Kane, the housekeeper, to give him his lunch on a tray. Some rainy day, months ago, he had finished his solitary lunch, up there in his big study, lined with books on history and art and architecture, that private den of his ringed with thousands of pounds worth of hi-fi equipment for the classical music he no longer listened to. She could see him making up his mind, then ringing his office and the shops and the building sites, saying he would not be doing any of his rounds that afternoon. One day, months ago, he had sat at the big partner's desk in the bay window of his study, and begun to plan all this, deciding what to do on the holiday, ringing up London, writing letters, consulting brochures. Arranging all of it, even down to these roses on the table, doing it in secret, without one word to her or to Eileen. Planning to bring Eileen with them. A surprise. He liked surprises. He always had some sort of surprise at the parties he gave at home—a singer or special food or little presents for the women guests. A special treat, so that people in the town said: Oh, if you're ever invited up to the McAuleys' house, Tully-more, oh, it's great, lashings of food and drink, and always some sort of entertainment, and they have a band for dancing. Money's no object there. You'll have a good time. Money was something Bernard made plenty of, but didn't care about: it was a means to an end, although God knows what Bernard's ends really were. She some-times wondered if he knew himself. But until Eileen came along, no matter what he took up, no matter what new interest occupied him—music, getting up plays for the Liskean Players, traveling abroad, going to picture galleries, reading history, the building sites—nothing satisfied him for long. And since Eileen, all that was for-gotten. He had never wanted anything the way he wanted Eileen. There would be no stopping him, no dealing with him now.

"Coffee, Mona?" He had poured it for her. She took

her cup and went to the window of the suite. She heard the tone of voice in which he talked to Eileen. Casual, friendly, but not terribly interested, the way a husband might talk to some girl who was a friend of his wife. Eileen had no notion. But Mona knew that tone: he spoke as though he and the girl were alone in the room. Mona looked out at the small garden which the hotel called the Garden Court, a bedraggled set of rose bushes around a rectangle of wet green lawn on which a large ginger tomcat stalked a sparrow. The bird seemed not to see the cat, but as the cat bellied closer the sparrow flew straight up into the gray London sky. She wondered what he would have done if she had refused to go to London with him. For, of course, he could not bring the girl on his own. She remembered, a few months back, when they were first supposed to go to London, the two of them, he had told *her* to go on her own. He didn't want to go. And she had gone on her own, except that at the last minute she bought a ticket not to London but to Brussels, where she had never been. She looked up at the gray sky and remembered the Plaza Hotel in Brussels, the record playing on the record player, and herself laughing as the words were translated to her. *Madame est servi.* She brought the record home with her. A souvenir.

Bernard was saying something about Harrods and now he called out her name. "Mona?" They were asking her a question. She came back from Brussels as from under an anesthetic, turning to them with a ghost smile that warned him she had been far away. He understood that smile. He repeated what he had said.

"I was just saying, Mona, that tomorrow morning we might all go to Harrods. I know you want to look at those goosedown duvets for the big bed and we should show Eileen their cosmetics department."

"Harrods. What time?"

"Well, would ten be all right? Would that suit you? I thought afterward we might have lunch in that wine bar in Sloane Street and then I'll take Eileen off for the afternoon to the Tate."

He was waiting. Answer him.

"All right," she said. "Harrods and lunch. But after that I'll be engaged."

"Fair enough." He turned to Eileen. "Mona has a friend here, a girl she went to school with. Trouble is, I don't get on with her, do I, Mona?"

"She's my friend," Mona said, and left it at that.

"Who is she, would I know her?" asked stupid Eileen.

"No, I don't think so. She's a girl I knew when I was at Queen's."

"That's right, it wasn't school, it was Queen's," Bernard said. "Anyway, Mona goes off to see her on her own."

"Oh, it will work out somehow," Mona said. "You show Eileen the sights, that's what you enjoy doing, isn't it, showing people the sights? The trouble with me is, I've seen all the sights. But we'll work it out."

"Of course we will," he said.

At 10:45 Bateman brought the Jaguar Sovereign back to the hotel. The doorman on duty was the same one who had helped him unload the luggage earlier, a fellow Geordie. So Bateman waved to him and pulled over in front of the taxi rank. "I'm picking up that party again, all right?" he asked the doorman, who gave him the nod. He got out and said good morning to a chauffeur he knew who worked for the Davis Group, then went to wait by the front steps. After a while the doorman, his fellow Geordie, joined him. "Got you all day, then, have they?"

"They booked till midnight. My relief comes on at six."

"I know that party," the doorman said. "Mr. McAuley. Irish. Comes here a couple of times a year. With the wife." The doorman laughed suddenly. "He's all right," he said. "He'll look after you." And went off to open a taxi door for an arriving guest. Bateman looked at his watch. It was just on eleven-thirty. As he did, he saw them come out of the front entrance above him, the bloke rigged out in a pinstripe suit, then the young bird, only a kid, really, and the wife, a smashing-looking blonde she was; smashing legs. He went up to them. "Morning, sir, morning, madam." The young bird smiled at him.

There was a bit of discussion then about who should sit where. "Maybe Eileen should sit in front, she'll get a better view." "No, Bernard, let her sit in the back with you. You can point out the sights." And so it was that the smashing blonde got in the front with Bateman, and there they were bowling along up Birdcage Walk past the Horse Guards barracks and this party telling Bateman directions like a bloody tour guide. Bateman, pretending to check his left-hand lane, looked down at the legs beside him.

"Driver," said the party in back, "if you go down to the Mall now, I think we'll be just in time for the noon Changing of the Guard. Can you park somewhere near the palace?"

"I could drop you in front of the palace, sir, and come back to pick you up, whenever you wish. But there's no parking spot near there."

"All right, then. What did you say your name was, by the way?"

"Bateman, sir."

"All right, Bateman, we'll do that. Is that okay with you, Mona?"

Beside Bateman the wife sighed to herself quietly, so quietly that Bateman didn't think the husband heard her. "Wait," she said. "Maybe I have a better idea. I'll drop you and Eileen off at the palace and use that time to take the car up to Conduit Street for a minute. There's some eyeshadow I could pick up at Dior. I'd love to have it for tonight."

"But would there be time? What do you think, Bateman?"

Bateman thought this husband was the worrying sort. "I imagine we could do it, sir."

"I've seen the Changing of the Guard so many times," the wife said to no one in particular.

"All right, then. But, please, don't be too long. Remember, our lunch booking is for one."

"Don't worry, I won't be late."

And so Bateman drove them down the Mall and let him and the kid off at Buckingham Palace. The usual mob of tourists was clustered around the railings and perched on the statues at the Victoria Memorial; they reminded him of pigeons. He pointed out a spot near Birdcage Walk and arranged to pick them up there. And the next thing was, as he drove back up the Mall with the wife sitting beside him, she said, "Bateman, what's your first name?"

"It's Arthur, madam."

"Arthur, I'll tell you what. I don't think I'm going to have time to go up to Conduit Street after all." She laughed. "I just didn't want to watch those soldiers stamping around like that. You're English and I know the English are very proud of all these ceremonies. Aren't you?"

"Some are. Yes, madam. But I can't say I'm particular."

[17]

"Oh, good. I didn't want to annoy you. Look. Why don't you just find a quiet street where we can park and wait."

"Very good, madam. Would you like to stretch your legs? I could stop up ahead and let you off and come back for you in, say, fifteen minutes."

"No. Isn't there a quiet street near here? Think."

So he drove on, turning into Carlton House Terrace. It was quiet with a small private park, no traffic to speak of. Big houses, private staffs. He parked near a Daimler. The Daimler's chauffeur was having a smoke and keeping an eye on two little Arab kids who were running around and banging on the park railings. Bateman heard the chauffeur shout at them and realized he was minding them. Christ, what drivers had to put up with, nowadays.

"Will this do, madam?"

Mona McAuley looked back down the quiet row of elegant mansions, at the little private park, the chauffeur of the other car shouting at those children. No one walked the street. She turned and looked behind. The street was empty. She looked at the young driver. "We have the car just for today, is that right?"

"That's right, madam."

She turned in her seat, facing him, tucking one leg up under her. She looked into his face then, slowly, looked down at his dark uniform suit, clean white shirt, black tie, the narrow black trousers. "You don't mind waiting here, do you?"

"No, not at all, madam."

"Arthur."

"Yes, madam."

"Nothing. I just said your name. Just to get the sound of it. Do you like your name?"

Bateman looked at her. Was she having him on? "Never thought much about it, madam."

She smiled. She leaned her head back on the leather

headrest, smiling at him. "I like it," she said. "It's a nice name. Arthur. It suits you. Did you know it suits you?"

He felt himself color. "No," he said. He did not say "madam."

At lunch in Overton's Restaurant Eileen had to go in first, it was polite for them to put her first, but if they only knew how she hated that, for the headwaiter advanced directly on her, his watery eye suspicious, as though she were alone and had no right to come in here. And so she turned, awkward, back to the McAuleys for help. Bernard came up at once, spoke, and the head-waiter waved her on, and again she found herself at the head of a procession of three, following the headwaiter's broad back past a seafood bar and a sort of anteroom where men sat drinking sherry, into the dining room proper, with its cut-velvet banquettes and tables set with white linen and flowers. When they took their seats Bernard mentioned champagne he had ordered in advance, and the headwaiter, pleased with himself, indicated that it was already in an ice bucket at the table. The headwaiter signaled and an Arab-looking waiter came forward and poured the champagne into tall, narrow glasses, the sort Eileen felt she might easily knock over and break. Smoked Scotch salmon and Dover sole cooked in various ways were discussed by the McAuleys and the headwaiter, who then left large menus for further consultation and went off, followed by his Arab subordinate. "Arab waiters in Overton's," Bernard said crossly. "Things have changed."

"So have the customers," Mona said, her eyes going to a party of Japanese men in black suits. The McAuleys began to read the menus and talk about what might be good. Eileen carefully picked up her glass and sipped the champagne. She had only had it once before and that was at Mona's thirtieth birthday party last Christmas. It tasted bitter. She put down her glass very carefully, then took up the menu. Mind your manners, miss, her mother's voice said in her head. Don't stare over your teacup like a cow looking over a whitewashed wall. Knives and forks are laid the way you're meant to use them. Go from the outside in. If you don't know something, watch your hostess.

"What would you like?" Bernard asked Eileen.

"Oh, you decide. You know best."

"Mona," he said. "What do you think?"

Mona said maybe Eileen would like turtle soup, but Bernard said no, maybe she should have oysters to start. Did she like oysters? She was not sure. Anyway, she would like what they would like. "No, no, what would *you* like?" Bernard asked her again, and to gain time she picked up the tall glass and, nervous, drank down the rest of the champagne while staring at the menu. The Arab waiter came up behind her and refilled her glass, although she said no. Bernard was pleased by this. He said that Arab waiters seemed to be an improvement on English ones but that France was the only country where waiters really knew their jobs. Then he said, "Well, Eileen, what have you decided?"

"I don't know. What are you going to have, Mona?"

"Well," said Mona. "I think smoked salmon to start and then a grilled Dover sole on the bone."

"I'll have the same," Eileen said.

"But are you sure?" Bernard wanted to know. "I mean, there are lots of other choices."

Which was easy for him to say, but Eileen didn't know what some of the dishes meant, for all that she had been good at French in school. And besides, there were no prices on her menu.

"No," she said. "That sounds nice. Smoked salmon and then grilled sole."

"Well, all right, then," Bernard said, at last. He called the waiter. Eileen sipped champagne, relieved that the choosing was over. The McAuleys began to reminisce about some black sole they had eaten in the west of Ireland. Once they got into this sort of chat Eileen was not expected to contribute anything except her ears and a few polite exclamations of interest. The McAuleys had been to lots of places and liked to talk about them. On their honeymoon four years ago they had been to Italy and Greece, and since then they had been several times to France and once to Spain, and they came to London about twice a year. Lismore is a hole, Bernard would say in a high, gleeful voice. It's a rotten wee hole and no self-respecting person should have to live in it. And then he would give his mocking look and say, But if you quote me to anybody at home I'll put my solicitor onto you. Eileen had asked him if he had always felt that way about Lismore and if he had, had he ever thought of going to live someplace else? And he said, Didn't you know, I've been corrupted by money. Oh, it happened quite early. Would you believe, he said, that I used to be a pure sort of a lad, a young fellow with ideals? Would you believe that while I was at Queen's doing my B.Sc., I suddenly wanted to give it all up and go away and give myself to God. Yes, the priesthood. But the minute I mentioned this vocation of mine at home, my dear old father came right up through the floorboards in a cloud of smoke like Beelzebub, buying me a brand-new car and lashing out pound notes for me to spend weekends in Dublin. And I fell. Yes, at the tender age of nineteen, I became a fallen angel. I went over to Mammon. And here I am today. Fallen and a failure. But of course he was no failure, everybody knew that. His big mud-spattered Mercedes was out on the road every morning, winter and summer, driving down into Lismore, then over to Crosstown and back to Lough Kean, where he had building sites, sometimes off on the forty-mile trip to Belfast in the afternoons, and almost always back to Royal Street and the big shop before closing. And Eileen's mother, when Eileen told her what Bernard had said about being a fallen angel, said it was nonsense, she said Bernard couldn't wait to take over the father's business the day he left university, because by then the father, who was a widower, was drinking in a big way and letting things go to rack and ruin while he ran around with some woman up in Belfast. And she said Bernard had worked like a Trojan reorganizing and expanding the shop in Royal Street, fixing up the pubs they owned and buying a business in Crosstown and another shop in Liskean, until by the time he was thirty and married Mona he was the leading Catholic business-man in the district. Failure, *moryah*! said Eileen's mother, who was a Donegal woman and an Irish speaker and admired men who were good at business as Eileen's father had never been.

The McAuleys were still talking about black sole. Then the waiter came up and the talk died down, for the McAuleys must look over everything they were of-fered: the slices of smoked salmon, the thin slices of brown bread, buttered and served in a silver dish cov-ered by a white napkin, the fingerbowls with lemon wedges in them, and as the waiter poured the rest of the champagne, Bernard told him he would like to see the wine steward. It seemed to Eileen that the McAuleys were now in better humor than they had been when they left Belfast this morning. Maybe it was because they were in an expensive place making sure they were treated right. That was what they liked. They were so particular. Bernard, in particular, was particular. Eileen, feeling the champagne, smiled to herself. She thought of the ceremony she had just seen with Bernard, the Guardsmen marching up and down, the officer with his drawn sword, and the regimental bands playing away in the palace courtyard. She was in London, abroad at last, drinking champagne, seeing Buckingham Palace, being driven around in a chauffeured car. With the McAuleys. As usual, anything really super that happened was because of the McAuleys. Life was funny that way. Everything was an accident. When her mother became ill Eileen had been planning to do nursing in the autumn of that year, but had to find a job at once to replace her mother's earnings. And Father Higgins, their parish priest, said he would speak to the McAuleys. A job in a shop had not been Eileen's idea of what she wanted to do with her life, nor was now, but that was what she got. And while working in a shop was a bit of a drudgery, hours of rearranging dresses and sweaters on racks after people had pulled them out, things like that, still, if she had done nursing she wouldn't be sitting in this restaurant today. If Mona McAuley hadn't taken a fancy to her, none of this would have happened. And that was an accident. Mona of all people, Mona who was so beautiful and sure of herself, not the sort Eileen would have thought would make a friend of the likes of her.

"Enjoying yourself?" Bernard leaned across the table, smiling at her, thinking she had smiled at him. "Enjoying your holidays?"

And they all three laughed, for Hugh Burns, who was the manager of one of Bernard's pubs, always said that to the English tourists. "Enjiing yer holidays?"

The McAuleys tasted the smoked salmon. Bernard pronounced it perfect. The wine waiter came up and Bernard consulted the wine list. "The Meursault, sir? Very good, sir. Full bottle?"

"Yes."

"Oh, none for me, I'm drunk already," Eileen blurted out, but the McAuleys laughed and exchanged amused looks. They were not stiff with each other now, the way they had been earlier; they seemed more the way they had been when they took her to Dublin and gave her three super days in the Shelbourne Hotel, taking her to the Abbey and to expensive restaurants. Oh, you could get accustomed to this sort of life with no trouble at all. And in Dublin Mona had taken her into some of the big shops and introduced her to the people who ran the cosmetics and the junior-fashions departments, people Mona knew. And when she introduced Eileen she would say, "This is a girl I'm training for big things." And Bernard had been very nice, too; she'd never spent any time with him before, but in Dublin he really put himself out, spending hours and hours taking her around, showing her all the sights.

The waiter poured the wine. Bernard tasted it and then the waiter filled their glasses. "Try it, Eileen," Bernard said.

She tasted it. It too seemed bitter. Dry was what they called that. "It's lovely," she said. "But I'll be drunk if I drink it."

"Nonsense," Mona told her. "Anyway, I want to propose a toast." She lifted her glass. "To this week," Mona said. "To enjoying our holidays."

Wednesday, August 27

On the morning of her fiftieth birthday, Agnes Hughes got up at seven. Without Eileen to help her it was slow work dressing. Not that she was complaining. She did not believe in going on about what ailed her. She had noticed when she was in the hospital that if you are sick you are like a story in the newspaper. After a day or two your troubles are no longer news.

As she raised the blind it stuck and she had trouble unraveling it. Outside, it rained. She looked at the familiar brick chimney of the Ulster Linen Works, the slate roof of Danahar's Garage, and the narrow entry leading up to the Dublin Road. The refuse bins in the entry were overflowing. The binmen had not come. These days there was always someone on strike. She heard the rumble of a heavy lorry on the Dublin Road and then a cock crowed on a hill outside the town. She loved the sound of cockcrow. It made her think of her childhood on a farm in Donegal. She went to the chair by the bed and put on the surgical stockings they had given her at the hospital. Two years ago, just when she was about to set off on the big trip of her life, a visit to her son in Canada, she had come down with a heart attack. She had had a second attack last year. But she was still hoping to get to Toronto. She was feeling better. She knew she was.

When she had finished with the surgical stockings, she put on the rest of her clothes. She slipped her feet into slippers, but, remembering it was her birthday, went to the wardrobe to get proper shoes, then sat at the dressing table to fix herself up. The gray was coming back in. She must get out to the hairdresser soon. She brushed her hair, then put on powder and lipstick. Her sister, Maeve, was coming to see her later today and she wanted to look well for her. She was going to make a casserole and Maeve would be bringing a birthday cake. Now she examined her face, giving it the sergeant-major inspection that good-looking women use on themselves. For she had been a beauty; had known it from the time she entered the Mater Hospital in Belfast as a seventeen-year-old student nurse. First it was medical students grabbing hold of her in the wards at night when the nuns were off duty, then the staff doctors flirting in the clinics with the assurance of men who thought they were gods. She had resisted all of them: there was something arrogant about medicals, something she didn't like. Instead, she had married a nice boy from home, a schoolteacher, but soon found out that he could have done with a little of that medical arrogance. He was too nice. As her uncle, the priest, said of him once, "He was a lad who lay down on the highway of life." It was true that he accepted a job in a parochial school when he was qualified for something much better. He died of leukemia when he was thirty-eight years old. He had no pension. She had to go back to work as a nurse to support the two children. Now, she could work no longer. Since her heart attack she had been dependent on

Eileen's pay and the little her son, John, could afford to send her from Toronto now that he was married and starting a family of his own.

When she had finished doing her face, Agnes Hughes went downstairs, taking a good hold on the banister as she went. Pain is normal, it's a warning, and it's not necessarily something for you to be alarmed about, the doctor had said. And the other doctor, the specialist at the Royal Victoria Hospital in Belfast, had told her she should try as far as possible to lead a normal life. That was what she was trying to do. And maybe next spring, if she kept on improving, she would finally get to Toronto. She went down carefully and along the back hall to the kitchen. The kitchen looked out on a narrow back yard, with a ten-foot-high brick wall around it. She had put geraniums in pots to cheer up the yard, but the trouble was the sun had to fight its way in there. Twenty-three years she had lived in this house and could count the days you didn't have to switch the light on in the kitchen. She switched it on now as she went in. The kitchen clock said ten to eight. Eileen would probably ring early. Anyway, no need to worry about hurrying to the phone. Eileen knew it took her a minute to get there. She had thought of her daughter a lot these past days, thought of her away there in London. London and New York and Paris were the places Eileen dreamed about, and now she was in London with the McAuleys, who would show her the best of everything and make her fall in love with it altogether. She was lucky, wasn't she? But, on reflection, Agnes Hughes did not think her daughter was lucky. All this holiday would do would be to make her pine to go to London and live there. Which she can't do with me around her neck. She's not lucky, Eileen, she never was lucky. She was born at the wrong time. Ever since she was old enough to go out and play, there's been no playing in the streets here in

Lismore. Nothing but British Army patrols and searches and bombs and shootings and burn-outs. And, going on these fifteen years, nobody goes out at night. Children used to be able to go off after teatime to play with their friends in one another's houses, and girls used to go off to dances, you never worried so long as they weren't home too late, so long as some boy didn't have them off up a lane. It's not boys the people worry about now: I wish it were. It's bombs and bullets. And the people don't see each other the way they used to: the old life is gone forever, everybody stays at home, stuck up to the telly, you never go over to your neighbor's, is it any wonder there's more drink and tranquillizers than ever? And Eileen's not the way I used to be; even if things were all right, she doesn't make friends the way I did when I was her age, poor Eileen. It's my fault, I suppose, for I wanted her to have a good education, that's why I sent her to the nuns in Ballycastle as a boarder, for I was there myself when I was a girl. I liked the nuns at Ballycastle and the convent never made me shy. But it made Eileen shy, it cut her off from boys. She's a bit on the tall side, but she's good-looking; she takes after our side of the family in looks, but she's not like me, not one bit. If I was in a place like McAuleys, meeting people all day long, I'd soon get over being shy with boys. But she hasn't. Oh, good and all as the McAuleys are to her, it's not the right place for Eileen, working in a shop. It's my fault, for getting sick. Eileen deserves better, her father was at the university, and Johnny too. For one thing, what sort of boys does she meet working in McAuleys shop? It's a very ordinary class of boy she'd run into there.

In the kitchen, when she had wet the tea, Agnes Hughes sat down with the library book she was reading. At eight, the factory whistle from the Ulster Linen Works deafened her, as it always did. At eight-fifteen she heard the special high whining sound of a British Army Saracen armored car as it went down the street on its regular morning patrol. At eight-thirty the milkman put a full bottle on the doorstep and took away the empty one. Then, next door, old McDevitt started up his Morris Minor and left for work. The sounds of the morning were like clocks striking, doling out the hours and half hours of her day. When she had cleared the breakfast dishes she went into the front sitting room. Most days she spent half an hour doing exercises from the chart Dr. McCaslin had given her, but today was her birthday so she declared a holiday. Later she would bake the casserole, but not until Mrs. McTurk, her char-woman, had been and gone. She heard the Belfast train go through the cutting at the end of the town, the en-gine driver blowing his whistle the way he did every morning except Sunday, when there was no train. Maybe she should do her exercises after all. She remem-bered the shock she felt the morning she came home from the hospital in Belfast. The nurse had taken her into the hospital bathroom to give her a proper bath, and for the first time since the attack she had seen her-self naked in a full-length mirror, the skin hanging in folds on her body, she had lost so much weight. Still, since the exercises, it was coming back to a more normal look. But you had to keep at it. By next spring, when she'd be ready to go to Toronto, she hoped most of that slackness would have gone.

What time was it, anyway? It must be after nine. The television set stared at her, showing her her own face in its screen. It would be nice to have television in the mornings the way her son said they had in Canada. A person couldn't read all the time. Still, she liked read-ing. She sometimes said where would she be without books. So now she read, waiting for the telephone to ring.

When it did ring she warned herself there was no need to hurry, but old habits die hard, and she was short of breath by the time she reached the front hall and picked up the receiver. "Hello?"

"Hello, Mama, it's Eileen."

"Oh, sure I know it's you. It's nice to hear your voice, dear."

"You miss me, then?"

"Of course I do, but I'm all right. How are you?"

"I'm grand. Has Mrs. McTurk been coming?"

"Yes, yes, everything's going well. Now, tell us about London. Are you enjoying yourself?"

"Oh, Mama, it's great. Listen, happy birthday!"

"Thanks, dear. Well, what about London? Start at the beginning."

"I will, I will. But, first of all, Mona and Bernard said to wish you many happy returns of the day. And they said not to worry about the phone bill, but that I was to ring you up as often as I wanted."

"Oh, that's very nice of them, but you mustn't do that. Anyway, be sure to thank them for me, won't you?"

There was a silence on the line.

"Eileen?" she said. Suddenly London seemed very far away.

"I wish you were here, Mama."

"You're not the only one. So, tell us, how're you getting on?"

And listened then, trying to remember everything Eileen told her so that she could tell it later on to Maeve. Ever since the heart attacks, she worried that she didn't remember things the way she used to. That's nonsense, the doctor said, your memory's not affected in the least, but she did forget; maybe it was the tranquillizers. Still, as Eileen talked she got nearly all of it fixed in her mind, the chauffeured car that first day, the lunch at some place with smoked salmon and champagne, and then tea at the Ritz. (Would you believe it, my daughter that I gave birth to in Drumshane Hospital, she's having tea at the Ritz in London?) And then to the Royal Something for a play and supper at another restaurant. And then, yesterday morning they went to Harrods, and in the afternoon Bernard took Eileen to the Tait, was it? Anyway, a gallery to look at paintings. And then last night, Eileen said, they went to an Italian restaurant, "just the two of us."

"You and Mona?"

"No, Bernard and I."

"Well, where was Mona?"

"Well, that's it, she didn't come with us. It seems she knows some girl here in London, someone Bernard doesn't like, and so Mona goes to see her on her own."

"I wonder who that would be."

"I don't know. But it's going to be the same carry-on today. He's taking me to a place called Kenwood House this afternoon and tonight to another play and supper. And he says Mona won't be with us tonight, either."

"Well, that's funny, isn't it?"

"Do you know what I think?" Eileen said. "I think they're having some sort of row, the pair of them."

"The McAuleys? Oh, go on, sure they always get on the best."

"Anyway," Eileen said, "there's something funny. But I tell you, Mama, it's a bit wearing being alone with him all the time."

That was a thing that worried her about Eileen. She was like her father, she never knew when she was well off. "Oh, come on, now," she said to her. "Bernard's very nice. He's very kind. Anyway, if he and Mona are having some wee tiff, that's their business. In the meantime, they're giving you a lovely holiday."

"I know. You should see the prices he pays. Listen, what I wanted to tell you is that when you hang up, you're to go into the sitting room and open the bottom bureau drawer. I have something there for you."

"Oh, now, you shouldn't have."

"Nonsense. Happy birthday. And listen, I'll ring you Thursday."

"All right." Suddenly she felt lonely. "Well," she said. "Have a lovely time, dear. You'll be home on Sunday evening, then?"

"Yes. Goodbye, Mama."

"Goodbye, dear. And thanks for the present, whatever it is."

As she put down the phone, thunder banged in the sky above the house. Thick, fat raindrops smudged the kitchen windowpanes. Eileen in London, chauffeured around. She went to the bureau her husband used to sit at long ago marking schoolchildren's exercise books and preparing lectures for his classes at Holy Cross School. She opened the bottom drawer as Eileen had told her. Inside was a big packet wrapped in red paper and blue ribbon, the paper they used for wrapping gifts at McAuleys shop. She took it out and put it on the table in the middle of the sitting room, pleased but worried, for what if it was something she didn't like or need?

A raincoat; a trenchcoat. She looked at the label. A Burberry; it must have cost a lot of money. I wonder, did she get some sort of discount through the shop, through Mona? Mona has all sorts of connections in commercial circles. Anyway, it's lovely, very stylish, and a lovely red-and-black-plaid lining. I never had one this nice before. She put it on and went to look in the oval mirror. She stood inspecting herself, turning slightly to the right, then to the left, then turning her back to the mirror, peering over her shoulder. And the thought that came to her was that she did not look right in it. It was not the coat's fault, it was her fault. She was too old for it.

A key turned in the front door and she heard it open with a loud, dragging sound. Then Mrs. McTurk's heavy step in the front hall, her voice calling: "Morning, missus, are you down yet?"

"Yes. Good morning." Foolish in her finery, she turned to face the intruder.

"You're not going out in that rain, are you?" was the first thing Mrs. McTurk said as she came in the sitting-room doorway.

"You mean the coat? No, it's a present from Eileen. I was just trying it on."

"It looks lovely on you," Mrs. McTurk decided. "Have you heard from her yet?"

"Yes. She's having a great time." There was no sense going into details with Mrs. McTurk, for if you did, she would stand talking for an hour and the floors would not be done.

"Isn't it well for them, this generation," Mrs. McTurk said, leaning up against the doorway. "I mean, in your day and mine, missus dear, Irish people only went to the Continent once in a lifetime, a pilgrimage to Lourdes or Rome. And now they're off at the drop of a hat, the way it was a day excursion, only it's the Costa Brava or someplace like that. Sure, my wee nephew Sean, he's only an apprentice, but he's been every place. Greece, he was in last summer. But isn't it great for them, though?"

"Yes." Agnes Hughes began to take off the new raincoat, carefully, planning to put it back in its box.

"It's a lovely present, that," Mrs. McTurk said. "A good raincoat, mind, that's something a body can always use. I wish we could use them a bit less. Did you hear the thunder a while back?"

"Yes. Oh, by the way, Mrs. McTurk, there's a new

packet of Lux under the kitchen sink. You said you wanted more Lux."

"Aye, so I did." Annoyed, knowing she was being dismissed, Mrs. McTurk went down the hall to the kitchen. A few minutes later she turned on her little pocket wireless, awful music, but what could you say to her; anyway, it was better than having her waste the morning standing here missus-dearing you to death with her yarns about her relations.

Agnes Hughes put the raincoat back in its box, folding it as it had been folded in the shop. She wondered if Eileen was right and the McAuleys were having a falling out. She doubted it. Mona had her head well screwed on. She wasn't the sort to annoy her husband by yelling at him. Agnes Hughes had known Mona's family on both sides: she remembered Mona's mother well, a big streel of a woman, the daughter of a police sergeant, pretty when she was young, who married Mona's father when she was living up in Belfast. He was a dentist with a sort of a practice in Lismore, but whatever it was about him, he never seemed able to make much of a go of things. Mona was their only child. They lived in a wee flat over his surgery in Kent Street, which was a row of small shops at the bad end of the town. It was hard to believe that Mona had ever lived on Kent Street, looking at her now, so poised and rich-looking in her beautiful clothes, and living in that big house on Clanranald Avenue. Of course, she was well enough brought up, she qualified as a chemist, doing her training in Dublin and then coming back to Lismore to work as a pharmacist in Crowleys The Chemist's. She was always a lovely-looking girl, and Agnes Hughes remembered hearing that she had half the boys in Lismore chasing after her when she went to work in Crowleys, and then remembered hearing the yarn about how, a couple of years later, Mona got engaged to that young barrister from Lurgan, what was his name? and they said he broke the engagement off when he found her flirting with his best friend. Then she married McAuley. Could it be something like that that was causing the trouble now? Ah, I doubt it. Sure everybody says they're really close, they get on the best, always have. They don't run around with any particular crowd in Lismore, they keep to themselves off there in Clanranald Avenue and go on all those holidays together, and sure he trusts her like his own self, by the sound of it. Didn't he as good as turn over the running of McAuleys shop to her? She was the one who engaged Eileen and later gave her the rise in pay. Oh, she's a far step now from Kent Street, the same Mona. Or even from making up prescriptions in the back of Crowleys in her white coat. I have a notion, though, that she's lonely living up there in that house, with nothing to do, a maid and a housekeeper and what have you. Running a shop has nothing to do with having a real home. They have no children, the McAuleys. They say Mona doesn't want them.

Is that the doorbell? Damn old McTurk and her music.

"Mrs. McTurk? Mrs. McTurk? Is that the doorbell?"

But Mrs. McTurk did not answer, the music still blaring away in the kitchen. It could be the postman with a parcel, and postmen never waited, they rang twice and left. Agnes Hughes got up and half ran out to the hall. When she opened the front door there was a delivery boy outside.

"Mrs. Hughes?"

"Yes."

She knew the boy's face, he worked for Collins, the florists. He handed her a long box and then a second box, also wrapped in gift paper. The second one looked like chocolates. "I was told to deliver this as well," he said as he gave her the second box. And she had to tell him to hold on a minute, going back into the sitting room, the damn music still playing in the kitchen, to get her purse and go back and tip him. And then, breathless with all the hurrying, feeling a twinge of pain in her chest, she took the two boxes back into the sitting room and put them on the table. She opened the box of flowers. There were twelve yellow roses. She took the card out of its tiny envelope.

FROM THE MCAULEYS
Many Happy Returns

Yellow roses were her favorite flower, she had said so to Eileen the last time she was in the hospital, and the next day two dozen had arrived from the McAuleys. And they had remembered now. She bent over and smelled the roses' fragrance. Then she unwrapped the other box. Chocolates. Would they be from Maeve? But when she opened the box and saw that they were handmade truffles from that Swiss shop in Belfast, she knew they were not from Maeve, who could not afford them. The card read:

HAPPY BIRTHDAY
Mona & Bernard

The McAuleys. The McAuleys, who weren't even friends of hers, sending her two expensive presents on her birthday and all because of Eileen. In the kitchen the music stopped, and Mrs. McTurk appeared in the sitting-room doorway, wiping her wet hands on her apron. "Was that the door, missus?"

She said yes, it was.

"I never heard it. They must have only rung the once." Nosy Mrs. McTurk approached the box of flowers. "Roses. Who are they from? They're lovely. Will I put them in a vase for you?"

"Yes, please." But she took the card out of the box

before handing it over to old McTurk. It was none of her business who they were from.

"And chocolates! Presents galore. Is it your birthday or what?"

And suddenly she thought, It's the McAuleys I have to thank for all these presents, the flowers, the chocolates, and even the coat, for Eileen never could have bought it without Mona's help. It's them I have to thank for my birthday, people I hardly know, people who hardly know me. And that, for some reason, made her feel like crying. "Yes," she said, and heard a catch in her voice. "Yes, it's my birthday."

When Eileen rang her mother that morning it was from the hotel lobby, because there was no phone in her attic room. After the phone call she ate alone in the hotel lounge. The McAuleys never ate in the morning, just took black coffee in their suite. Eileen had a big breakfast, bacon and egg and toast and tea. Afterwards, she was to go around the shops with Mona while Bernard kept an appointment with his tailor. In the afternoon, as she had explained to her mother, Bernard would take over and show her around while Mona went off to see her friend.

At a quarter to ten, when she was sure the McAuleys would be up and ready, she rang their suite. The phone rang six times before Bernard answered. "Seven-five-six," he said, in his business voice. "McAuley here."

"Bernard, it's Eileen. Is Mona ready yet? I'm not too early, am I?"

"No, no." He sounded distracted. "Eileen's on the phone, Mona," he called. "Mona?"

There was a wait. Then he said, "She's just coming. How are you? Did you ring your mother?"

"Yes."

"How did she like the coat?"

"Oh, she hadn't opened it yet. I just told her there was a present for her in the bureau drawer. I wanted it to be a surprise."

"Oh, I see," he said. He still seemed distracted. "Here's Mona."

Mona came on. "Eileen?"

"Yes, hello. I'm not too early? I can call back later, if you like."

"No, no," Mona said. "The trouble is, I have a head-ache. A hangover, to tell you the truth. I was out last night with these friends of mine and I drank too much whiskey. Anyway, I have a head the size of two. Look, would you mind if I reneged on this morning? I'm only fit for bed."

"No, that's grand." And it was grand, in a way, for now she would have a few hours on her own. "I'll just wander around for a while on my own."

"What?" Mona said. She didn't seem to hear. "Wait a minute, Eileen." Eileen heard Bernard call out something, she didn't catch what it was, and then Bernard came on the line. "Look, Eileen, how would you like to come with me to my tailor's? It won't take more than a few minutes and then I'll be free to do whatever you like."

"No," she said. She felt her voice panicky. "No, honestly, Bernard, I'd just like to go off on my own for a while."

"Ah, you're only saying that."

"No, I'm not. Listen, I'll meet you at lunchtime in the lobby as we arranged. All right?"

"No, wait."

"No, honestly," she said and hung up, astonished at herself for having had the nerve to cut him off like that. It was the first time she had ever done anything of the sort: he was her boss after all, and he was someone who expected people to go along with his plans for them. Still, the thought of being alone with him all morning and again this afternoon and this evening. Two whole days she had been here and never a minute to go off on her own. And it was a great feeling, wasn't it, to decide for once to do something the McAuleys didn't want you to do. But she had better get out of the hotel now, before he came after her to make her change her mind.

And so she went straight across the lobby and out the door, stepping into the street just like that first morning in London, not sure where she was. She looked around and saw the road she had taken to go to Buckingham Palace and then another road in the opposite direction which they had taken yesterday in the taxi to go to Knightsbridge. She turned in a third direction and began walking down past the big railway station. She passed by shops that had pictures of naked women in their windows, then entered a rotunda ringed by big pubs, and went down a road of sweets shops and luggage shops and little cafés, and into another road of what seemed to be small hotels with names like Chalmont Crescent Hotel and the Berkeley and the Victoria Palace and the Clarendon. The whole road was hotels on either side, hotels made out of converted private houses with Greek pillars at the doorways and iron area railings and big bay drawing-room windows. But all of these places were now slumgrimed, some painted a garish mauve or pink to hide the cracking plaster and broken front steps. Rubbish bins overflowed at the basement entrances and dirty lace curtains billowed out of open first-floor windows. And all around her, trudging up and down this street, were travelers, some of them young people with backpacks, but most of them Orientals and black people and Indians carrying heavy suitcases, which they rested after every block. They were the sort of travelers who never took taxis but carried their luggage to the nearest bus stop or underground. And that was why this road of hotels existed; it was a road of hotels for people who didn't expect much, just a bed to sleep in until they could get in touch with someone from home who would help them to get fixed up in some sort of job. There were no shops in the road except for a little corner grocery and, opposite it, a to-bacconist's. As she passed the tobacconist's window she saw that there were foreign newspapers for sale inside and in the window several little notices on a board, people offering to baby-sit, to teach foreign languages or give yoga classes, anything that would bring them in a little money while they waited in the Chalmont Crescent Hotel or the Berkeley, or the Clarendon. And as she went down this long road wanting to get out of it, it seemed to her that it was worse than the worst slums she had seen in Belfast or Dublin, for, bad and all as those places were, they were places where the people knew each other. But here in this road everyone she saw seemed shipwrecked, thrown up by a big wave into these dirty hotels amid a crowd of other strangers, all of them beginning again in this great city of London, which they had heard about all their lives. It made her feel afraid, this road, as though she were in one of those fairground mazes that are not frightening at first but become fright-ening when you start bumping into mirrors and finding yourself trapped. When she came to a crossroads, she turned into a new road which was like a mirror of the first one, terrace on terrace of dirty cheap hotels. Her step quickening almost to a run, she fled on past staring brown and black faces, past children playing in dirty areaways, until she came to a third, different street, with shops and familiar English products on sale. She walked more slowly now, not afraid, knowing she was lost but glad she did not have to retrace her steps back through those roads of hotels, those roads that were such a long way from the London the McAuleys had shown her, the London of uniforms and parades, of museums and palaces, of smart shops and porters carrying your suitcase and doormen opening doors and taxi drivers waiting, everyone as attentive as if you were the Queen herself.

And now, as she walked down the shopping street, the rain started, becoming a downpour, the sort that washes people off the streets. She stood in a shop doorway watching the rain spatter on gray pavement, thinking that if she were in London on her own it would be more like this: she would have a room in some cheap street, maybe sharing with another girl, and the only jobs she would be qualified for would be in a factory or a shop, someplace where you didn't need special skills. The rain wept in front of her. And what could she earn in a shop here, what chances of promotion would she have compared to what she had now at McAuleys? She thought of the big shop in Royal Street, aisles and aisles of it, cosmetics, of course, and next to that notions and then ladies' wear and then junior fashions, and the food department and stationery, and the alcove got up like a Spanish cellar, where they sold wine and cheese and gourmet foods. In the front was the men's department, and upstairs on the first floor were hardware and sports and fishing gear and plumbing supplies and furniture. It was the biggest shop for miles and people came specially into Lismore to shop there. And Mona had hinted a couple of times that "someday not too long away" Eileen might be given a chance to run the junior fashions and there was no doubt that if she stayed on at McAuleys and was still Mona's pet, she would rise fast, so that by the time she got married she'd have a really good job with them. And if she didn't get married? That was what you shouldn't be thinking about when you were only turned twenty. She looked out at the pouring rain, the gray London street. In the three years since she had left school, all of the girls she had gone around with, all of them seemed to have steady boy friends except for her and Bridey Kennedy. In Bridey's case it was because she was just too fat, although she had a pretty face. And what's my excuse? The only boy who seemed really keen on me was Dan Mallon, last summer, and maybe that was because he was home on his holidays from training as a vet in Dublin and had no girl in Lismore. Anyway, the first two times he asked me out he was very nice, I thought he was serious, he drove me to Belfast for the pictures and supper, and then the third time it was to go to a dance with him up in Liskean. He must have had eight pints of porter that night before he ever met me and then walked all over my feet at the dance, and on the way home, at one in the morning, he pulled his car into a lay-by and kissed me, and when I kissed him back he unzipped his pants and took out his thing and asked me to touch it, and when I wouldn't he tried to grab me and then had to jump out of the car all of a sudden to be sick all over himself and all over the road. Why is it that the boys I'd like to ask me out are shy, or not interested in me, and seem to avoid me when I try to be nice to them, and boys that you know, all they want is grabbing you and trying to pull your pants down, they don't care who you are, they'd do it to any girl who was fool enough to let them, they're the ones who wink at me at the corner of the street, or come into the shop and annoy me, or follow me home from work and ask when are you going to give them a date.

She stood, waiting. The rain continued, so heavy there was no chance of running for a bus. She heard a church carillon, a loud beautiful peal unlike any church bell at home. And then the chimes, slow and solemn. She counted them. Eleven. Eleven, and if it kept on raining this hard, she would never be back and changed and ready at twelve to meet Bernard in the hotel lobby. He hated people to be late.

A taxi passed with someone in it. Then another with its light on, and to her own surprise she ran out and waved it down. She had never taken a taxi before except to get her luggage to a station or to take her mother home from the hospital or the doctor's, and when the taxi stopped she felt a worry about how much it would be. It was being with the McAuleys that had made her do it: the McAuleys would have done just what she had done, got a cab without thinking about it. That was it: it was easy to get into the habit of being like them, and if you did, could you ever go back to the old days? But it was nice, sitting in her own taxi. In ten minutes she was back at the hotel, home and dry. The fare was not as dear as she thought it might be. She tipped the driver. Wouldn't it be lovely to be rich.

At the hotel she changed, did her hair, and was downstairs in the lobby with twenty minutes to spare. Yesterday, Bernard had told her that the plan was to have lunch with Mona in some pub and then he would take her off on his own to this Kenwood House. But if Mona was still under the weather, would she get up and come out to lunch? And at the precise moment that she was wondering about Mona, she looked up and saw Mona come out of a lift and walk quickly across the lobby toward the front door. Eileen got up to go to her, but as she did, Mona went out through the door with the doorman, and the doorman ran down the steps whistling for a taxi. Eileen stood, looking out at Mona, who waited, wearing a coat and carrying an umbrella. She watched the taxi come up, watched Mona get in, and then turned around and went back into the lounge. She sat again in the same chair as before, facing the lifts. At twelve, Bernard had not come down, he who was never late. At ten past twelve, a lift opened and he came out in a hurry among a stream of other guests. He was dressed in a gray plaid suit and carried a neatly rolled umbrella. He looked worried and cross. She at once came out of the lounge and went over to him.

"Oh, there you are," he said. "Sorry I'm late. I was keeping poor Mona company upstairs and I lost track of the time. Anyway, I've ordered her a sandwich and some soup. I'm afraid she's not up to coming out with us."

She looked at him. How easy he was with a lie.

"Do you think it will clear?" he asked as they went toward the front door. "I imagine you didn't have much of a walk in that rain." He pushed the revolving doors, indicating that she precede him. As they came out, the doorman blew his whistle for their taxi. It was no longer raining but was chilly and overcast. "I'm sorry about Mona," she said as they stood there watching the taxi come forward from the rank. He did not answer her, except to say: "Here's our taxi."

"Where to, sir?"

"The Grapes."

The doorman repeated the address to the taxi driver and they were off.

"Is she going to stay in bed all day, then?" Eileen asked.

He leaned back on the cushions and put his thin claw hand up to his face, pressing his fingers against his shut eyelids. "I don't know," he said in an exasperated voice. Then, as though pulling himself together, he sat up straight on the taxi seat and smiled at her. "Well," he said. "And where did you explore this morning?"

"Oh, I just walked. As a matter of fact, I got lost and

[44]

in the end I had to take a taxi back. It's the first time in my life I ever took a taxi just to get home in time."

He laughed. "Is that so? That's what I love about you."

"What do you mean?"

"I don't know. It's—it's that you're such an innocent."

That offended her. "Well, and isn't it well for me, then, that I'm such an innocent?"

"It is," he said and laughed again. "It is, indeed."

The taxi was now driving along terraces of huge cream-colored mansions through a square with iron railings enclosing a little private park. In sudden excitement, she recognized that this was a part of London she'd seen on the telly. "This is where they had *Upstairs, Downstairs*," she said. "With Hudson, the butler, and Lady Margaret."

"That's right. Yes, this must be it. Although I think it's mostly embassies and offices nowadays."

And now the taxi stopped on a little street off this square and let them out at a pub which was not like the pubs at home. For one thing, all the people in it were more the sort you'd find in a hotel bar, young men in suits with vests and a few model-ly-looking girls in see-through blouses. They and the young Englishmen were the sort who, if they knew you worked in a shop, they would turn their backs on you. The minute she went into this pub she wished she were someplace else, but Bernard led her forward, confident. "Look at the two at the bar," he said in a quiet voice.

He meant two old ladies sitting on high bar stools, one of them in a velvet trouser suit with a vest and a white shirt with a silk bow tie. Bernard went right up and stood by these two old ones and ordered drinks in his harsh, confident, Ulster accent. She saw the old ladies give him a look and half turn their backs, making it clear that he was not their sort. But of course Bernard was not annoyed by that. That was one thing she admired about him, he never let himself be downfaced by anybody, he acted in any place as though, if he took the notion, he might buy it any minute, lock, stock, and barrel. Now he started in, telling her a story about a drunken wedding reception he had once been to near here in the Irish Club, which he said was a fine big house in Belgravia, and he began about how the bride's family were from Achill Island and were Irish speakers and were told, mistakenly, that the club belonged to the Irish government. And when they got very drunk and obstreperous and were asked to behave themselves or leave, they said they would do neither, because this place belonged to the people of Ireland and so it was their own place, and by God they would bloody well wreck it if they wanted to. Bernard had a great way of telling a story, doing the accents of the Achill people, and she drank Dubonnet, which she liked because it was sweet, and after a while she was no longer uneasy at being among these stuck-up English ones. For the first time that morning she was enjoying herself. Maybe it wouldn't be too bad spending these days in London with Bernard, he wasn't a bad stick, at least he put himself out to amuse you and you could learn a lot by listening to him; he didn't talk like a businessman, he was more like a teacher, teaching you things. Her father had been a teacher, but she didn't really remember him. He died when she was eight and the only thing she remembered him teaching her was how to swim. Her older brother, Johnny, who was now in Canada, said that their daddy was a hard man and beat him with a strap. But she didn't remember that. She sometimes wondered what her mother thought of their father. Had she loved him? She never mentioned him at all, these last years.

Now, when they finished up their drinks, Bernard took her into the back room of the pub, where there was a woman giving out sandwiches and salads from a little counter. They had to queue, and he left her in the queue while he went back to the bar for a couple of glasses of wine. It was then that she thought of Mona going out of the hotel and Bernard telling that easy lie about Mona still being in bed.

"Tell me," she said, when he came back with the wine, "why am I such an innocent?"

But it was their turn at the food counter, and being Bernard, he had to arrange that first. "What about Scotch eggs?" he said. "And that ham looks all right. Would you like ham and tomato salad? Or what about that potato salad?"

And so when they had chosen and he had paid and tipped the woman (the tip must have been big, for the woman hurried to exchange their paper napkins for linen ones, which she took from under the counter), they went back into the larger pub room. "Why am I such an innocent?" she asked again.

"Are you? Sure I know nothing about you. Maybe you have a secret life."

"Maybe," she said. She thought of Mona going out of the hotel. "But that doesn't answer my question."

"You're unspoiled," he said. "You mustn't ever lose that. It's your great secret. Tell me. How was your mother when you talked to her this morning? I suppose she hadn't got our flowers and chocolates by the time you rang?"

"What flowers and chocolates?"

"Oh, a few roses. It's yellow ones she likes, isn't it? And we sent her a few truffles from Savatier's."

"Oh, God, Bernard, you shouldn't have done that. That's awfully nice of you."

"It's nothing. It's her birthday. And she must be missing you."

Yellow roses. Chocolate truffles from Savatier's. She

saw the dark sitting room at 19 Church Street, the florist's box of roses, the expensive chocolates, the new raincoat laid over a chair and her mother and old Mrs. McTurk looking at it all. "Oh, missus dear, them is lovely, was it Eileen sent you all that? Ah, now, children stand to you in your age, so they do. Oh, is it Mrs. McAuley is the roses and the sweets? Oh, very nice." And her mother nodding. I hope Mama likes the coat, she'll know it was Mona who got it for me. Poor Mama, she'll be keeping the coat good so that she can wear it when she goes to Canada. If she goes.

"Eileen," Bernard said, "don't look now, but in a moment take a peek at our two friends at the bar."

She looked up at the two old ladies. The one in the velvet suit had her hand on the other woman's knee, caressing it. "What is it?" she asked. "Is there something I'm missing?"

"What are they?"

"What do you mean, what are they?"

"They're lesbians, of course."

She stared again.

"A couple of Ellen Morrisseys," he said, and laughed.

"What do you mean, Ellen Morrisseys? She's not! God, she's never off her knees, she's at Mass every morning. I see her going down the Dublin Road every morning as I'm getting dressed."

"Ellen Morrissey is a lesbian," he said. "Everybody knows it, except you, it seems. Ah, well. I said you were an innocent."

He stared off across the room as though he had thought of something else. "But of course," he said. "God is an innocent. The gods aren't interested in the sins of mortals, or the loves of mortals. That's one way they differ from the rest of us."

She wanted to say, But isn't God supposed to care about our sins, to care about every one of us? But he looked so strange she decided to hold her tongue. Whatever it was, she might not understand it even if he explained. She unfolded her napkin and began to eat the lunch. It's Bernard who's not like the rest of us, she thought.

Half an hour later, when they left the pub, it still threatened rain. A taxi took them up through London and let them off at the top of Hampstead Heath, where cold winds buffeted them as though it were a winter's day. Yet as they walked across the heath with several other people who were headed in the same direction, the clouds parted, releasing patches of sunlight. Moments later, as though Bernard had stage-managed it, the sun shone full and sudden on a splendid vista ahead, great green lawns, tall trees, an expanse of water, and, brilliantly white in the sunlight, the long façade of Kenwood House. Eileen stood enchanted. It was as big as any big house she had seen in Ireland, but open, not hidden by high stone walls, standing unimaginably grand in its own park in the middle of London. At the sight of it, Bernard gestured as though he were offering it to her. "Well," he said, "will that do you?"

"Oh, God, is that it? Whose is it?"

"Yours and mine. It was built by Adam, a famous English architect, for Lord Mansfield, the Lord Chief Justice of England in 1767. And it was given as a gift to the English nation in 1927. And paid for, if I may say so, by pints drunk by the Irish nation."

"But how was that?" she asked, although she was not really listening. She looked at this great house and saw it as a house in a book, its dark, handsome owner riding his chestnut hunter across these lawns at a canter, coming to ask her, the governess of his motherless children, if she would take tea with him that afternoon in the drawing room.

"The Iveagh Bequest," Bernard was saying. "The Guinness family bought this place and gave it to the British people." And then, as they came closer to the house, he began to talk about something called Palladian architecture. She remembered once, when he was explaining some buildings to her in Dublin, she had asked if he studied architecture when he was at Queen's. "No," he said. "It was just something I read up on to fill the empty spaces. Do you know what I mean? Something to fill up the days. Anyway, that's all over now, my life is full. It's perfect." But what was his life, what did the McAuleys do at home when they were not working? Although they lived right by Lough Kean, they didn't sail or fish, like other people in their crowd. Anyway, what was their crowd? In the year and a half she had known them, she had never heard them talk of any special friends. If they gave parties they were always big parties for twenty or thirty people, doctors and lawyers, and business people and the big farmers. They had both Catholics and Protestants at their house, but they didn't go around with any group that Eileen knew of. For instance, they never drove over to the Garron Towers Hotel for drinks and a meal on Saturday nights, as most of the top people did. They weren't in the golf club, and apart from the time Bernard had produced plays for the Liskean Players, they never took part in any local do's. They were both only children and seemed to have no close family. They never went to cousins' weddings the way other people did. In fact, when she thought of it, Eileen didn't know what they did do, once they had finished work. She could just see the two of them sitting in the big dining room in Clanranald Avenue with the housekeeper serving them dinner. But what did they do after dinner? Telly was what most people were stuck into now-adays, but Bernard didn't like telly. She supposed Mona watched telly while Bernard studied and read books. Maybe they went up to Belfast a few times a week, but she doubted it; nobody, even the Belfast people, liked being out in the city at night, what with car searches and not being able to leave your car unattended in case someone shoved a bomb in it. Mona enjoyed working in the shop, that was obvious, but did Bernard enjoy working? He must, otherwise how could he say his life was perfect? Eileen thought of Bernard's day and all the people he had to see, starting off in the morning at his building sites, then maybe driving out to Crosstown to go over receipts with his pub manager, then having lunch with someone, maybe one of his suppliers, in the Garron Towers Hotel, and afterward, sometime in the afternoon he would usually drop in at McAuleys in Royal Street. That was when he often had a word with her, chatting with her as he did with his other em-ployees. But yet, when you talked to him, he never talked about his business, not ever. He would talk about anything, the weather, a football match, plays, or tell a story about some place he had been to abroad, but never business. In fact, he was the sort of man, if he hadn't come into the business through his father, he might have been something else entirely, maybe a university lecturer or something like that. In the time Eileen had known him, he was always instructing her. Just as now, when they went inside Kenwood House, he began to point out paintings by Rembrandt and Gainsborough and Vermeer. She would have loved to have been able, as he was, to stop in front of this paint-ing called *The Guitar Player* and tell about the interiors in Vermeer's paintings and explain how it was thought that Vermeer had used some optical instrument to help him get such a crystal-clear mirror image. And then he took her to see a beautiful library room. They weren't able to go inside it but stood at a rope barrier with other tourists, looking in. Bernard pointed out that the room had an Adam fireplace and said the ceiling decorations were by an Italian called Zucchi. She stood looking up at the handsome Greek pillars, the gilt-framed mirrors, the gold and white and blue decorations, the worn pink carpet, the leather-bound books in their niches. Real people had once sat in this room and read those books. Rich people. Lord Mansfield. People who were born rich and stayed rich. "Oh," she said to him. "Wouldn't you give anything just to live in a place like this."

Of course she didn't really mean it, it was one of those things a person says, she could no more see herself drinking a cup of tea in this room than she could see herself asleep in bed in Buckingham Palace. But when she said it, Bernard became completely still. The other people at the rope looked in at the room, then moved on, but Bernard did not move, he stood as though he had been shot. Then, when the people had gone, he turned and looked into her face. There was something in his look that made her afraid. It was as though she had said something terrible.

"Do you mean that?"

She nodded, what else could she do, it was so strange the way he stared at her that she knew she could not say she had been half joking. He reached out and took hold of her hand. "Let's go outside."

"But don't you want to see the rest of the rooms?"

"Later. Come on."

He pulled her after him, keeping a tight hold of her hand. It was not like him. He was her boss, and married and older, and she had noticed at other times when a person might touch you or take your arm, he seemed to avoid touching her. But now he pulled her along, down the gallery of paintings and out of the house altogether, onto a terrace with park benches where you could sit and look down on the great green lawns. He marched her to an empty bench and, letting go of her, ran his hand along the seat to make sure it wasn't wet. "Sit down," he told her.

She sat. What was the matter with him? Above her the sun went in behind dark clouds and a great black shadow slid across the clipped lawns. In the year and a half she had worked for the McAuleys she had never seen Bernard so agitated. Of course, Mona was the one she knew best, Mona was the one she worked for and who had given her the job and was good to her and fond of her. Bernard had always been kind and very nice, but he was the husband, probably nice to her on account of his wife. Yet now he kept staring at her as if she had committed a murder. As if he was afraid of her. And as he sat down on the bench and looked at her, it occurred to her that he was behaving like a person who was not right in the head. He didn't seem able to control his movements, and for a man who was normally tidy and even a bit of a dandy, he was suddenly a sight, with his thinning brown hair sticking up behind, showing the bald spot he normally concealed. His dark eyes were nervous and skittery, and he glanced about him, as though somebody was about to attack him. "What is it?" she asked. "Did I say something? What's the matter? Tell me."

"Yes, you did say something." He turned from her and stared down at his shoes, his narrow beaky face seeming gray and cold under the clouded dark sky. "It might be significant, what you said. I think, maybe, you gave me a sign. It could be an epiphany."

Epiphany was a word she wasn't sure of: it was a

church holiday, wasn't it? She didn't remember what had happened at the feast of the Epiphany. "Epiphany?" she said. "What do you mean?"

"You said you would give anything to live in a big house like this. You said it without any prompting." He leaned back now and looked up at the sky, resting his narrow shoulders against the back of the bench. "Oh, I'm moving into dangerous waters," he said. "I know it. Silence is the rule, it's the only way. One must never speak. And yet if the gods offer an epiphany, does that mean I'm being tested and must ignore it? Or does it mean that I must act? Oh, I suppose I loaded the dice a little for this response by bringing you here." And suddenly he laughed in a wild way and, turning to her, slapped his knee like a man making a point in an argument. "I'm just like old Barney," he cried. "Just like my old da." And then, imitating his father's thick country accent: "Look, boy, go out in the drive in front of the house and you'll see something that will interest you." And he hooted with laughter. "Remember? When he gave me the new car."

"I don't understand you," Eileen said. She felt uneasy and embarrassed by all this mad laughing and carrying on. When a person older than you suddenly began behaving in a wild way, it was awfully awkward. It wasn't even as if he were drunk.

"Of course you don't understand, it's my dilemma, not yours. All you did was give a sign. All right, maybe you did and maybe you didn't, but anyway, after what you said, I have to tell you this much. But first of all, it's a secret between you and me. You mustn't say a word to anyone. Not even Mona. Especially Mona. Promise?"

"But what?" she said. She did not like the idea of

having secrets with him that his wife didn't know about. But maybe it was some surprise he was planning for Mona. He loved planning surprises.

"No. First you must promise," he said, staring at her with intense eyes.

"Promise," she said weakly.

"I'm buying a house," he said. "Oh, not as big as this, but a very big house, with grounds and stables and dozens of rooms."

"You're joking. Sure you have a big house already."

He shook his head. "Oh, no. Not like this one."

"Where is it, then; is it in Lismore?"

He laughed. "That hole! No, it's in County Louth. It's called Dunloe. It was built in the eighteenth century by one of Cromwell's officers, some murderer who got paid off in Irish land. His son added to it, quite a bit. It's basically a Regency house."

"In County Louth. Would you keep your own house, then?"

He ignored this. "You should see it. It was used as a stud farm in the thirties and it still has stables and a show ring. And a gate lodge, and an avenue leading up to the house, nearly a mile long with huge old beech trees. And the house! Wait till you see it. It even has a ballroom." He stopped and stared at her, shiny-eyed, as though drunk. "There used to be fifteen hundred acres with the place, but the land's been sold off. I have thirty acres. Enough to keep it private. It's all part of a plan. And you're part of the plan."

What plan? What did he mean? "But how could you live in County Louth?" she said. "What about your businesses and the shop and the pubs and all that?"

"It's not that far," he said. "And I could sell our house in Lismore tomorrow at a very good profit.

There's a business I'm interested in near this new house. I'm negotiating to buy it. It could be a big thing. It's a jam factory."

But all she could think of was what plan, why was she a part of it, why was he telling his private business that he hadn't even told his wife, to her who was only a junior employee and no relation to him?

"Listen, Bernard," she said. "It's none of my business, but why haven't you told Mona? Are you planning to surprise her or what?"

He turned on the seat and looked at her in that strange, frightened manner. "Oh," he said. "This is the Rubicon, isn't it?"

"What do you mean?"

Swiftly he put his hands up and covered his face with his long fingers as though he had a sudden headache. "The Rubicon," he said. "And I've crossed it without even thinking. Oh, my God. I hope I'm right."

She waited. She tried to remember what the Rubicon was. Wasn't it a river in a poem? Something she had learned in school and forgotten. She saw him uncover his face, and again he looked at her. "Don't you know?" he said. "No, of course you don't. I have been perfect. Perfect until now. You haven't the slightest idea of what I feel about you, have you?"

"No," she said. She felt her face flush. She looked down at her hands and, in a sudden nervous gesture, slipped them under her knees. She wished he had never started this. She wished he would say nothing more.

"You are the most important person in the whole world to me," he said. "You are my secret. I know you'll not understand this. I suppose I don't want you to understand. Maybe I never should have spoken. Maybe I should have kept my vow of silence. I'm putting everything in jeopardy by saying even what I've just said." He leaned toward her and took hold of her wrist and pulled her hand out from under her knee. He held her hand in his hands. She tried to take her hand away. It was awful. It was Mona who was her friend, not him; it was Mona who was fond of her, not him. And how could he say the like of this when he was married to a lovely young wife that everybody thought he was lucky to have got. What was the matter with him?

"Oh, go on, you're joking," she said. "You'd better be joking." She tried to laugh, maybe she could laugh it off; if he had any sense he would laugh too and pretend it was all a joke.

"I'm not joking," he said. "I bought this house for you."

When he said that, she pulled hard and freed her hand from his grip. She got up off the bench, but he grabbed hold of her again: it was awful. "Sit down," he said, like some mad person. She sat down. Maybe he *was* mad. They say you often don't realize it when a person is mad. "Let me explain something," he said, staring at her in that frightened way that frightened her. "I'm not going to hurt you. I'm not going to touch you. I'll never touch you or bother you in any way. I swear to God, I'll never even take your hand like that. You don't have to worry. Listen, sex isn't love. I know that. It's the opposite of love. Love, real love, is quite different from desire. It's like the love a mystic feels for God. It's worship. It's just wanting to be in your presence, that's enough, it's more than enough, it's everything there is. That's what it's been like for me since the first day I saw you in there, working in the shop. I've worshipped you. In silence. In devotion. Eileen, are you listening?"

She nodded. She looked at her shoes. She couldn't look at him.

"Then, today, suddenly, you said you'd like to live in a big house. And, of course, that's been part of my plan. My secret plan. Because, in true love, to be with the person, to be in their presence, that's everything. And so I thought, Maybe this is the moment, maybe this is the time to tell her my plan."

"What plan? What are you talking about? Why tell me some plan you haven't even told Mona?"

"Is it Mona that worries you? Don't worry. Mona will love to have you."

"What are you talking about, what do you mean?"

"I mean my plan is for you to come and live with us in this new house. You'll have your own suite of rooms. You'll even have your own car."

"You're mad. What about my job, what about my mother?"

"Wait. Remember you said once that your mother would love to live in Belfast with your aunt if only they could afford it. I'd buy a flat for the pair of them."

"And what about me?" she said. "What am I supposed to do in County Louth? Dance around in the ballroom of your big house?"

"I'm going to put you in charge of the office in this jam factory I was telling you about. I'll pay you twice the money you get now."

"But I don't want to work in a jam factory. I don't know the first thing about running an office. In fact, I don't even know if I want to go on living in Ireland."

"Ah," he said. He stood up, looked at her, then walked a few paces down the path. He stood for a moment with his back to her, then came up to her again. "Of course," he said. "Of course. Why didn't I think of that? You're here, you're getting your first look at London. And you want to see Paris, you've always wanted to see Paris. And the last thing you want to hear about is being shut away in some house in the country in Ireland, no matter how lovely it is. It *is* lovely, this house, by the way. Very lovely. I know you'll love it. But, never mind, it's not the moment. I was dead wrong. I never should have brought it up."

She looked at him then, looked him full in the face for the first time since this had started. "All right," she said in a low voice. "Let's just pretend you never said it."

He nodded. He turned away up the path again, walked a few paces, then came back. "I just wanted to say one more thing. If you trust me, you can go to London every year for a good holiday. And Paris, too. That's a promise."

"Will you please stop talking about it," she said. She stood up, felt herself shaking, whether with anger or fear or disgust at what had happened, she did not know.

But he moved around in front of her, thrusting his beaky features at her. "Listen," he said. "You could go on your own. You wouldn't have to go with us. London and Paris, all expenses paid. Listen, Eileen, listen. You can trust me. I'll never mention this again. It's been nearly two years now since this happened to me. Yet you had no idea. I didn't say one word to you, did I?"

"What have you said to Mona?" she asked, for if he was going to hurt her, she would hurt him back.

"Mona?" His dark eyes skittered around as though looking for Mona. "Never mind about Mona," he said. "This is between you and me, not Mona."

"That's not true," she said. "Mona's my friend." There was no getting out of it now. It was awful. He had spoiled that friendship, he had spoiled everything.

"All right, then," he said. "All right. We'll not speak any more about it. It's all my fault. I broke the rule I set for myself, the rule that made what I feel right and true and perfect. I've destroyed it. But if you could pretend to forget what I said, then I'd have that little bit of hope to hold on to. So we'll try to forget it, will we? Will we do that, then?"

She nodded, not looking at him.

"All right, do you want to go back in and see the rest of the rooms?"

"No," she said. "I want to go back to the hotel."

In the taxi he was silent for a time, and then began to speak about the play they had tickets for that evening, going on about it as though nothing had happened. She didn't say anything, she wasn't even listening, she was thinking about her mother, about phoning her mother, thinking she had to get somebody's advice about all of this. But how could she explain this to her mother? What good would that do? Worry her, that was all. As the taxi came up to the hotel, he leaned back on the cushions, closed his eyes, and said in a low, humble voice, "I'm sorry. Very sorry."

"It's all right."

"Am I forgiven, then?"

"Please," she said. She could feel the tears. "Please, you said you were going to forget it."

"All right. All right, then. Forgotten."

When the taxi let them off at the hotel she told him she was going up to her room. But when they came to the desk to get their keys, the Assistant Manager came out from his cubicle.

"Oh, Mr. McAuley. Glad I caught you, sir. We have a room for the young lady. It's a double on the Garden Court side, with bath, of course. Will that be all right? It's a double."

"Perfect," Bernard said.

"Any time you're ready then, miss, let the hall porter know and we'll send for your luggage."

"Will you have time to change rooms before the theater?" Bernard asked her. "Curtain's at eight, remember."

She nodded. She felt she couldn't speak to him.

"You'll have a phone now, so you can give me a ring when you're ready," he said as they got into the lift. "See you later," he said when the lift came to his floor. She went on up to the top floor and the little attic room. She took off her coat and hung it in the wardrobe. She should pack. But pack for what? To change her room or to go home? Sunday seemed a long way off. If she tried to go home ahead of time, she probably wouldn't get a flight, they were all booked up at this time of year. Besides, Bernard had her ticket.

She counted the money in her purse. She had only fifteen pounds on her. She had spent all her extra money on the raincoat for her mother. In London, she'd known the McAuleys would pay for everything, the way they had in Dublin. She had depended, as always, on the McAuleys. She sat down on the bed and looked up through the dirty skylight at the evening sky. How can I go out with him this evening and sit through a play with him and supper after? If only there were someone to talk to, someone who could advise her. How could she tell Mama this story, Mama who was always saying for her to be nice to the McAuleys, who thought, as she had, that Mona was the reason Bernard was nice to them? But there was nobody she could ring up, nobody even that she could borrow her fare home from, except Aunt Maeve, and it would be even harder to get Aunt Maeve to believe this than it would be to get Mama to believe it. No, there was only one thing to do. Go on, and pretend that nothing had happened. She got up, went to the wardrobe, and packed her suitcase. She left it where the porter would see it, then locked the room and went downstairs to tell the hall porter.

When she reached the hall porter's desk, the tall boy was on duty, the good-looking one who had shown her the way that first day. "Hello there, miss," he said. He took her key and gave it to another porter. "Go up and get this young lady's case, then," he told the porter. He smiled at Eileen. "If you'll just take a seat in the lounge, miss," he said, "the porter will get your case and show you to your new room."

"Thank you." She smiled at him. If only someone her own age, some nice boy, would say to her what Bernard McAuley had been trying to say this afternoon. She went into the lounge. As she passed between the pillars at the entrance she saw Mona sitting at the far end of the lounge. Mona was the last person she wanted to face at this moment, and so, instinctively, she shielded herself behind the pillars. In the afternoons the hotel opened up a bar at the far end of the lounge. A few men were at bar stools at the bar counter, and other people were at small tables around the bar. Mona sat alone at one of these tables, a glass of sherry in front of her. She had not seen Eileen. Eileen, standing behind the pillar, could see that Mona was smiling at someone. But when she looked again it seemed as if Mona was smiling at no one in particular. And as Eileen watched, Mona turned a little in her chair, crossed her legs, and looked up at the bar where the men sat on bar stools, chatting. Eileen saw her look directly at a young man in a gray suit who was sitting all alone at the end of the bar. Mona smiled at this man. The man did not notice at first and then he did notice. He did not smile back at Mona but looked at her as though she had mistaken him for someone else. Then, as Eileen watched, Mona sipped her sherry, put her glass down, and looked up again at the young man. And again she smiled a large, welcoming smile. This time the young man looked at her and gave a very small smile in return. He picked his drink off the bar and went over to join Mona at her table. He sat down. Mona smiled at him, then said something. The man said something and pointed to Mona's glass, but Mona shook her head as if to say she did not want a refill. The young man then finished his drink and signaled to the waiter to bring him another. He and Mona talked some more. Mona smiled a lot. The waiter came with the young man's fresh drink. Then Mona said something to the young man and stood up. Eileen, afraid of being seen by Mona, retreated even farther behind the pillars. She could no longer see Mona or the young man, but in a moment she saw Mona out in the lobby, talking on the house telephone. Eileen looked back at the young man, who had drunk his drink in a hurry and had his wallet out and was trying to get the waiter's attention. Then, a moment later, Mona passed Eileen's hiding place, going back into the lounge to rejoin the young man. The young man could not get the waiter and so put some pound notes on the table and stood up, ready to leave with Mona. But Mona said something and he sat down again. Then Mona came out into the lobby a second time and stood, facing the lifts. As Eileen watched, Bernard came out of one of the lifts, nodded to Mona, and went straight on out through the front door of the hotel. Mona turned around, went back into the lounge and up to the young man, who had succeeded in finding the waiter and was paying his bill. When he had paid the bill, he and Mona went out into the lobby and Mona rang for the lift. Eileen watched the lift come, people getting out. Then Mona and the young man got in the lift and it went up. Eileen went into the lounge and sat down in the nearest armchair. She felt her legs trembling.

"Ah, there you are, miss," the tall young hall porter said. He was with the second porter, who had her suitcase. "This way, please, miss," the second porter said, and like a sleepwalker Eileen followed him to the lift, went up, was shown into a big double room with television and a view of the Garden Court. She remembered to tip the porter, and when he had left she locked the door and went to the window and stood looking out at the Garden Court. It was raining. She looked up, counting the floors, to the seventh floor, where the McAuleys had their suite. She did not know which windows were theirs. Some of the windows had the blinds down. She thought of Mona in the room with that young man, them taking their clothes off, Mona smiling at him, Mona looking at his sticking-out penis. She began to shiver and felt she would be sick. She went into the bathroom and stood over the washbasin, gripping its sides. A wave of nausea rose in her and she vomited into the washbasin. She ran water in the basin, than took a cloth and wet her face. She felt weak and dizzy. She went back into the bedroom and lay down, shivering. A weariness came on her and she pressed her face against the pillow. Shivering, hot and cold, she fell into a fitful sleep.

The phone.

She came up through sleep to stare around her at an unknown room. Where was she, where was that ringing phone? She remembered she was in her new hotel room and sat up, found the receiver, and lifted it.

"Eileen? It's half-past-seven. I'm in the lobby. Are you nearly ready?"

"I'm sorry," she said. "I should have rung you. I'm sick."

"Sick?" She could hear the dismay in his voice, could imagine him all ready, his overcoat on, tickets in his pocket, the restaurant booked.

"It must be something I ate," she said. "I'm sorry, but I'm not up to going out tonight. I think I'd better stay in bed."

"But if you're sick we must get a doctor to look at you."

"No, I'll be all right. Please, you go on to the play and I'll talk to you in the morning."

But of course, being Bernard, he did not heed that. "Never mind the play. Let me come up and see you for a minute."

"I'm not fit to be seen."

"Nonsense, of course you are. Look, I'm worried about you. Let me come up."

She knew there was no sense arguing. He would do what he wanted: the McAuleys always did. So she said, "Well, if you want," and heard him hang up. She got off the bed, took off her dress and stockings, put on her dressing gown and slippers, then pulled the bedclothes back as if she had been sleeping under the sheets. As she did, he knocked on the door. "Come in," she said, but had to go and unlock the door for him. Bernard, ready to go out, wearing his beautiful blue cashmere overcoat, a dark suit, white shirt and silk tie, rich-looking but uncertain, his dark eyes nervous, as though he was afraid of her.

"You poor thing," he said. "Get back into bed. Do you have a temperature?"

"I don't know. I don't think so."

"Go on, into bed now. You look very pale."

She obeyed him, got in, still wearing her dressing gown over her underclothes. He picked up the phone. "Suite 32," he said, and then: "Mona? It's me. Look, I'm in Eileen's new room. Number 203. The poor kid is sick and won't be able to go out tonight. Would you be a love and bring me down the medicine kit? What? Yes, now."

[65]

When he put down the phone he took off his beautiful overcoat and tossed it on a chair. "Is this my fault?" he asked.

She shook her head and shut her eyes, lying back on the pillow. If only he would clear out. But she heard him pull a chair up to her bedside.

"Anyway, I don't want you to think about all that now," he said. "I just want you well and enjoying yourself again."

She nodded, her eyes closed.

"Later, if you're up to it, I could order you a light supper here in your room."

She turned away from his voice and lay facing the wall. She heard him moving about the room. The blind was pulled down and the small bed lamp was turned on. There was a knock at the door. He went to open it.

"Eileen?" It was Mona. She turned and looked up at Mona, who was dressed as she had been in the lounge a while back. "How are you?" Mona said, and did not wait for an answer but put a thermometer under Eileen's tongue while Bernard unpacked aspirin and other medicines from a little black box that Mona had brought. "You're not going to the play, then?" she heard Mona ask Bernard. She wanted to speak, to say there was no need for him to do that, but she had the thermometer in her mouth, and when she tried, both of them shushed her.

"I have that dinner date," Mona said to Bernard. "No point in canceling now, don't you think?"

"I suppose not. I'll be here."

"All right. I doubt if I'll be home much before eleven, so don't wait up for me."

He did not answer that, Eileen noticed. Mona took the thermometer out and looked at it. "Normal," she said. "You'll live."

"Of course I will. A good sleep is all I need."

"Yes, best thing for you," Mona decided. "Well, all right, I'll see you in the morning, Eileen. I have to go now." And went out. Eileen saw Bernard follow her into the corridor, heard them whispering but could not catch the words. He came back in, closing the door behind him.

"Sleep well," he said. "Will I put the light out?"

"Yes, please." She watched him turn the bed lamp off. Then he sat down in the dark in a chair at the foot of the bed.

"You're not going to sit there in the dark with me asleep?"

"Yes, I am. And when you wake up, I'll order you a little supper. Maybe you'll be feeling better then."

"Bernard," she said. She sat up in the bed, desperate. "I can't sleep with somebody watching me. Now, go on. I'll be all right."

"Whatever you want," he said. He got up in the dark and went to the room door. "I'll look in later."

"No, go on out. Go to the play. I'll be asleep." But she knew he would not heed her. He shut the door behind him. When she was sure he had gone she switched on the bed lamp and got up, intending to lock the room door. But the key was not where she had put it. He must have slipped it in his pocket when he went out. Still, there was a chain on the door, which was better than nothing. She snibbed the chain, then switched the light off again, so that if he came by she could pretend she was asleep. She got back into bed, although she no longer felt nauseated. Instead, a dull guilt filled her as though she had done something wrong. There was no sense in trying to pretend that nothing had happened. It was pretending that had got her into this. She had known for some time now that it was strange that Mona had made such a pet of her. No one had ever made a pet of her before. She was lonely, she was shy with boys, she lived alone with her mother. And her mother saying it was because the McAuleys had no children; that didn't make sense, for they were married only four years and Mona was beautiful. But still, it had been easy to get used to Mona's presents and special discounts and the trip to Dublin and this trip, your air fare paid, drinks and posh restaurants, the best of everything, and everything free.

And all the time she had never guessed that it might be Bernard who was behind it. And who would believe that Mona would sit here in a London hotel making eyes at strangers and going upstairs with them? No, there was no more pretending possible. She could not stay on here any longer, she would have to tell him straight that she wanted to go home and ask him for her return ticket. She could pay him for the ticket later when she settled up and left the job. For there was no question of staying on in the shop. That was over.

She switched on the light, got up, put on her dress and stockings, and went into the bathroom to comb her hair and do her face. She was shaking with nervousness or determination, she did not know which, but the shaking made her do everything quickly, as though she were in a hurry to go off someplace. When she was ready she rang his suite. The phone rang and rang. What if he'd taken her at her word and gone off to the play? But just as she was ready to give up: "Yes?" Bernard's voice said. She heard loud television in the background.

"It's me. Eileen."

"Wait a moment." She heard the television set switched off. "What is it, Eileen, are you all right?"

"Yes, I'm all right. Listen, could you come down for a minute, I'd like to talk to you."

"I'll be there right away," he said, and hung up. He would take the lift. She did not know if she could keep her courage up that long, for the lifts were slow. She walked up and down the room, trying to rehearse what she was going to say. It crossed her mind to say she had had a phone call from her mother and that her mother wasn't well and wanted her home. Or had had a slight heart attack. But that was tempting providence, and besides, it was avoiding the issue. No, have some guts, she urged herself. Now's the time.

He knocked and tried to open, but the chain stopped him. She ran to release it.

"Oh, you're up." He sounded pleased. He had changed from his dark suit into a sweater and jeans. "And dressed," he said. "Grand. Are you feeling better, then?"

"Much better."

"Grand. Maybe we can go out and have supper someplace."

"No, I want to talk to you."

At once he seemed afraid, his dark eyes watching her as though she had turned dangerous. He sat on the edge of the bed, his long-fingered hands gripping his knee-caps. "Of course. What is it?"

She stood over him, looking down at his birdy face, his thinning brown hair, his dark anxious eyes. Bernard McAuley, the richest Catholic in Lismore, who had secretly bought a big house with her in mind, a house with grounds and stables and a ballroom. Bernard McAuley, who owned acres of farmland and a building firm and four pubs and the biggest department store in three towns, who all his life had had anything he asked for. And who now looked up at her as if he were a beggar and afraid of her, she who was only twenty, and had never in her life had power over anyone.

"I want to go home," she said.

"Why do you want to go home?"

"I'd rather not discuss it. I don't have the money on me to buy another plane ticket, so if you'd give me the ticket you have, I'll pay you for it later."

He unclasped his hands, flexed his long fingers, then gripped his kneecaps again. There was a silence which seemed minutes but could only have been the seconds it took him to digest what she had said.

He stood up. "All right. Do you want to go tonight?"

She was startled: no argument. She had not thought of going tonight, but now she nodded. At once he went to the bedside table and took up a telephone book. He looked up a number, then dialed and stood, the phone to his ear, looking at her. "They always keep you waiting," he said. His dark eyes, afraid of her yet reproachful, made her think of Caesar, a spaniel her mother once had, a dog always waiting to be walked but knowing you were not going to walk him.

"Still no answer," he said, and then she heard him say into the phone, "Hello? Yes, please. Yes. I was wondering, do you have a flight going to Belfast this evening? I see. And the other one is at nine. Would you have anything at all on that one? I want one seat. Well, what about cancellations, any hope of that? What? So you think, then, that there'd be no hope? No sense in going out to the airport just in case? I see. Thank you."

He put the phone down. "I was afraid of that. You know how booked up they are at this time of year."

"What about tomorrow morning?"

"Right," he said. "I should have asked about that. Maybe if we can't get you on a Belfast flight tomorrow, we'll try to get you on one to Dublin and you could take a train home from there. I'll ring them back now."

And so she waited while he got on the phone, waited while he waited by the ringing phone for the overworked clerks to answer his call. She went into the bathroom and collected her toothbrush and toilet things, then remembered that there was no chance of leaving tonight, so put them back by the basin. She could hear him on the phone asking about waiting lists. What if all the flights were booked up tomorrow and the next day too? She supposed she could take a boat home. She could not remember where the boat went from, was it Heysham? Heysham was near Liverpool. She would have to get a railway ticket and travel up through England.

She heard him call out something from the bedroom but didn't catch it. "What?" she called back.

"I'm going to try Aer Lingus now."

She listened. It sounded like bad news at Aer Lingus: the Dublin flights were as booked as the Belfast ones. She heard him put her name on the waiting list and give her room number and the phone number of the hotel. You had to admit he was doing his best: he was really trying. He hadn't argued with her, he had just gone ahead and was trying to help her. She was grateful for that. She had been sure he would try to persuade her to stay on. When she came out of the bathroom he told her he had her wait-listed on a BEA flight to Belfast at 11:30 tomorrow morning. And on the Aer Lingus flight to Dublin at 1:00. "You'll probably get on one or the other. All right?"

"Thanks, Bernard. Thanks very much."

"Not at all. Look, there's just one thing I'd like you to do."

She waited. Now for the catch.

"It's your last night in London, so why don't we go out and have a bite of supper? I promise you I won't talk about anything serious. Word of honor."

Well, when he said it like that, it was hard to say no to him. Besides, she had made her point, had faced up to him and won. All you had to do was make a stand and she had made her stand. She decided she would

[71]

say nothing to him now about leaving her job. She would go around to the shop when she got home and give her notice to the manager. Do it while the McAuleys were still here on their holidays. "All right, then," she said. "But some ordinary place."

"Right. There's a sort of wine bar down the street. I'll go and get my coat. Oh, by the way, here's your room key." He took the key from his pocket and put it on the table. When he went out she put on her coat, and it was then that she thought: I'm leaving London after only three days, going home to Lismore with no job anymore and Mama to tell, poor Mama, who'll not believe any of this. And then was glad that she was going out some-place this evening: anything was better than sitting here in this hotel bedroom brooding about all that had happened.

T he wine bar was only about three blocks from the hotel but Bernard insisted on taking a taxi because there was a drizzle. It was a noisy place, which she was glad of, and there was a youngish crowd there and the waiters seemed very jokey, and when Bernard got a table and ordered a bottle of white wine, the young waiter who brought it put the wine bottle be-tween his thighs and pulled out the cork with a loud plop, winking at Eileen. "There you are, dear," he said, splashing the wine in her glass. "Enjoy it."

"He's right," Bernard said as the waiter filled Ber-nard's glass. "Enjoy it, enjoy your holiday, what's left of it. Drink up." And lifting his glass, he drank it down in two swallows, then refilled from the bottle. "Let's see," he said. "There's a blackboard menu up there. What would you like?"

But she was finished with the McAuleys; now she

didn't have to pretend. "Anything," she said. "Something easy. Do they have hamburgers?"

"They have steaks," Bernard said. For once, he didn't seem to care about the food. "What about steaks and chips?"

"Perfect," she said, as he topped up her glass. "But be careful. Let's not get drunk."

"Drunk?" He held up his hands in a nothing-to-declare gesture. "When did you ever see me drunk?"

"No, that's true. But when you gave that party for the staffs I saw you get other people drunk."

"Did you, now?" He laughed. "Well, yes, it's sometimes a way of finding out the truth. *In vino veritas.*" And then, seeming in good form and not upset anymore, he told a story about an old lady who used to come to his father's house at Christmas and never said a word except how-do-you-do's and isn't-this-lovely and how he and his cousin had doctored up her sherry with vodka so that she became talkative and suddenly came out with a story about a man who had courted her in her youth when he had just come out of an insane asylum. It was a mean thing to do, getting an old lady drunk, and it shouldn't seem funny, but Bernard made it funny as only he could, and as he told it, laughing, he drank more wine and kept pouring and she had wine too, until, as the steaks came and the waiter put a bottle of red on the table, she saw that they'd finished the first bottle of white wine and that somehow they'd started on a second one. "Three bottles of wine," she said. "Wait! It's me you've made drunk."

"No, no," he said. "Anyway, what if I do, it's your last night. God, maybe I'll come with you. London will be no place without you."

"Oh, no, don't," she said, suddenly afraid.

"Ah, well." He stared into his wineglass. "Yes," he said. "I've made a fool of myself, haven't I?"

[73]

"We weren't going to talk about that."

"Yes. No politics at the dinner table. Yes." He poured red wine in new glasses. "Supposing I said I'd sell this new house and forget the whole thing, would that stop you leaving?"

Embarrassed, she shook her head.

"I don't mean just leaving tomorrow. I mean leaving us."

She looked at him, surprised.

"It's true, isn't it?" he said. "You're going to quit your job at the shop, aren't you?"

She nodded.

He picked up the red wine and drank some. He looked afraid again. "What will you do?"

"I don't know."

"Jobs are not easy nowadays."

"I suppose."

"I could help you."

"No."

"I mean, I could help you find a job some other place. Not working for us."

"I don't know what I'll do. I may go to Belfast. Or to Dublin."

"I see." All around them was the roar of talk and laughter, the noises of the bar, the hurrying young waiters balancing trays of food and drink. Bernard looked up as though he had seen something on the ceiling above him. His narrow features winced as though he were in pain, and as he stared at the ceiling, large tears fell from his unblinking eyes. She felt pity for him, a man crying like that in a public place.

"I might try to do nursing," she said, as though her talking would conceal the fact of his tears. "My mother was a nurse, remember?"

"Yes," he said. "Yes, so she was." He wiped his eyes with the back of his hand. He poured more wine in their glasses, although she gestured that she did not want more. "What am I going to do now?" he asked, as though he were talking to himself. "Take to the bottle like my father? Go into a depression? Kill myself?"

"You're not going to do anything of the sort," she said, alarmed. "Don't be silly, talking that way." She looked at his untouched plate, "Go on, eat something. It will do you good."

Instead, he drank again. "I was thinking of something I read once. Love is a religion whose God is fallible." He raised his wineglass and turned to her. "To my fallible God." He drank.

What did he mean? He made her feel stupid, saying things she didn't understand. "I never know what you're talking about," she said.

"Pay no attention, then. I talk a lot of rubbish. Eileen, dear Eileen, I was wrong, it's me's the fallible one, not you. You're perfect. I should have resisted temptation this afternoon. It's funny, the parallels between religion and love. They even have the same seven deadly sins. It was the sin of pride that did me in today. Wanting to impress you. Bringing you to London was another sin, the sin of gluttony, I suppose. Oh, Mona was right. I never should have brought you with us."

"Mona didn't want me to come?"

"Mona's very fond of you," he said. "She likes you a lot."

"But she didn't want me to come on this holiday?" She knew she shouldn't say this again, but somehow couldn't help herself. Mona was maybe the clue to this wild talk of his. Mona and her men.

"Mona?" he said, as though his mind were far away and they hadn't been talking about Mona at all. "Oh, Mona and I are another story."

"Mona didn't want me to come. There must have been some reason. Mona's very clever. She's much cleverer than I am." Suddenly she felt like crying herself. If only somebody else had told her he loved her.

He nodded his head. "Yes, she's clever. And beautiful. And she's done her best to make me happy. It's not her fault that things turned out this way. It's my fault. Because I only thought I was in love with Mona. That wasn't love, I know that now. Desire isn't love. Desire is something you can control. I mean, if I'd become a priest I'd have had to suppress it. It's not hard. There are ways. You can satisfy desire without making it a big part of your life. It's only when you desire some person in particular that you become dependent, as though that person's body is a drug. For a while, anyway, and usually you get tired of that body. But love isn't like that. When you fall in love with someone, really fall in love, it's a sort of miracle, it's almost religious. The person you love is perfect. As God is perfect. It's . . . I never felt this way about anyone or anything before. It's as though nothing will happen in my life that will have any importance from now on, compared to this feeling I have for you. It fills me. It leaves no room for anything or anyone else. It's all I have."

"That's not true. You have your work and you have Mona. You have a lot of people who depend on you."

"Depend on me? What do I care? I'm trying to save myself, not save the world. I told you, when I was twenty I wanted to be a saint, to save my soul, to love God, to do good. But it seems I wasn't wanted in that way. And, until now, I never knew in what way I could make some sense out of my life. I did everything I could think of: I married, I made money, I traveled, I studied, I tried to enjoy myself the way other people seem to do. But until I met you, until that day I saw you standing there in the shop, I never knew what real happiness was. I suppose you're laughing at me."

[76]

"I'm not laughing at you," she said. "But, please, you said you weren't going to talk about this."

"Yes, I did. But now that I've told you, let me tell you the rest of it. At home, when I wake up in the morning and know that some time during the day I have a chance of seeing you, either in the shop or just passing in the street, that's all I need. I live for that. I know that if I see you, for the rest of the day I'll be filled with a feeling of happiness. Complete happiness. And I want nothing in return. Do you understand?"

She nodded, although she did not. She felt her head dizzy from the wine. She could hardly hear him with the racket all around.

"I love you the way knights fell in love in medieval days. Courtly love. Do you know what that was?"

"I can't remember," she said.

"It was the impossible love, the love for a lady in a tower. Often the lady was married and honor forbade that the lover ever try to possess her. Sometimes he wouldn't even declare his love."

"I wish you'd remembered that part of it," she said, with an embarrassed laugh.

"Yes," he said. He leaned forward and stared at her. "Would you believe that I was never going to tell you about it. That I was going to go to my grave without saying one word. That was the secret of it all, the perfect thing about it. But having you here, so close, having you all to myself in London, seeing Kenwood, having you say that you wanted to live in a big house, it was too great a temptation. And so, I ruined it."

She bent her head and looked at her plate. She felt a wave of dizziness come and go.

"It would have been perfect," he said.

"It would not. I'd never have gone to live with you and Mona. Living with married people, what sort of life would that be?"

"If I hadn't been married, would that have made a difference? I know. You're only twenty and I'm thirty-four. I probably seem very old to you."

"Please," she said. "I feel dizzy. Could we have some coffee?"

"Of course," he said. He signaled a waiter and ordered two coffees.

"And eat some of your food," she told him. "It's getting cold."

"Yes." At last he took up his knife and fork. He cut the steak but did not eat it. "Let's talk about you. You said you want to do nursing. I might be able to help you with that."

"I told you, I don't want you to help me."

"Wait, now wait. Remember, I mentioned to you this afternoon about getting your mother a flat in Belfast, one she could share with your aunt. I could still do that. You could all three live in Belfast and you could attend one of the hospitals there. I'd help on the financial side. You could pay it back after you finish your training. It would just be a loan."

She said nothing. There was no need to get into an argument with him by telling him she would never take anything from him or Mona again. Tomorrow, with a bit of luck, she would be on the plane and away from them.

"What do you think? I could sell your mother's house in Church Street. I think I could get her a good price."

"I think I have to go to the bathroom," she said. She rose in sudden dizziness and went unsteadily among the close-packed tables to the ladies' room, where she stood in front of the mirror, dizzy, blacking out, then seeing her face floating in front of her. She waited until the wave of dizziness passed, then washed her face and tidied her hair. She was in the ladies room for ten

[78]

minutes. When she came out of the washroom and went to their table, she was chalk pale and shivering as though she had caught a chill. Bernard rose and drew out her chair for her. "Are you all right? Were you ill?"

She did not sit down. "I want to go home."

"Of course." Now at last he could be resourceful and help her, and he had her out of the restaurant in no time, paying the bill as he ordered a taxi. "Poor you," he kept saying. "Poor you. I think we'd better call a doctor."

"I'll be all right."

"Well, we'll just have to see about that. I'm not sure you should travel tomorrow."

"I'll be all right."

But when they got to the hotel he kept the cab. He said for her to go up to her room and he would go to a late-night chemist's and get some pills called Doxilan, which he said were great for nausea. "Just don't lock your door and I'll drop them off and you can take them before you go to sleep."

She didn't want to wait for him to come back but felt too sick to argue. When she got to her room, she undressed and put on her nightgown, still shivering and dizzy. When she got into bed and turned the light off, a wave of nausea rose in her, but she did not vomit. She felt weary then and dozed off, falling into a heavy, dreamless sleep from which she woke some time in the middle of the night. When she did, she felt a familiar dread, her old night terror that someone was in the room. She reached for the bed lamp, switching it on to reassure herself. There *was* someone. She caught her breath in fright.

He sat facing her, wearing his overcoat, his eyes unblinking, his narrow features giving him the look of a bird of prey. "It's me," he said. "It's all right."

"Oh, what are you doing?"

"Playing night nurse." He smiled. "I got you the Doxilan tablets in case you felt the nausea come back."

"What time is it?"

He looked at his wristwatch. "A little after two."

"Well, why aren't you in bed? Oh, go to bed, please."

"I'm not sleepy. And I love looking after you. Don't deny me that."

"No, but, Bernard, I told you before. I can't sleep with someone watching me."

"Of course you can. You were asleep just now."

"No. Please, go away."

"All right, then." He stood up. "Good night. Talk to you in the morning."

She watched him cross the room, watched him walking in an exaggerated tiptoe as though she were already asleep. And again, something about him, perhaps the way in which he hunched up his shoulders as though pressing invisible wings into his back, reminded her of a bird, a carrion bird, that narrow head, the beaked profile turning for one last look at her, and then a furtive wave of his long-fingered hand as with infinite care he let himself out and shut the door behind him. She lay, listening, to make sure he had gone. Then she got out of bed, went to the door, took the key, and locked herself in. She put the chain on the door. She went back to bed, turned off the light, and lay in the dark. She did not sleep.

Mona McAuley walked through the deserted hotel lobby, its only other occupant the night porter, who handed over her key. The public rooms off the lobby were dark. She passed by the lounge, where she had met tonight's first man. A disappointment, that one.

The second she had found in the Regency Bar in the Carlton Towers, an Italian who said he was an importer of woolen goods and who offered her money when she went up with him to his room. Sometimes she took money. It was, but not invariably, a sort of protection, legitimizing the encounter and preventing them from following after you or asking too many questions. Tonight, on hearing that the Italian was flying back to Rome in the morning, she had refused the money and told him to order champagne instead. Now she was feeling the champagne.

She liked the night, the late night of big cities like London and Paris, liked walking back alone through deserted streets to a hotel where Bernard slept or feigned sleep. It was understood he was not to speak to her when she came back. It amused her to walk into hotel lobbies and see the conjectural look on the face of the porter or desk clerk who handed her her room key: a pretty woman like her, out so late and alone. Sometimes, as now, those returning hours were hazy, their details forgotten in the morning hangover. She liked, too, the lift going up with her as its only passenger. She did not think of Bernard, did not even think about this holiday, except that tomorrow she would begin again. She would sleep off the champagne and go to Parke's Restaurant for lunch. The man from Tuesday night was to meet her there at one.

She tried to be quiet as she unlocked the door of the suite. But when she went in she saw that the lights were on, and in the bedroom, the bed, tidied by a maid since her last encounter, was not slept in. Was he up and at his eternal reading? But as she went on into the suite there was no sign of him. What time was it? The bedside clock said ten past two, would he have taken Eileen to some disco place? She undressed and came out into the sitting room and saw that the maid had forgotten to draw the sitting-room blinds. She went up to the window and stood, looking out at the dark, looking at whoever might be watching her, some man in his hotel room, alone, across the Garden Court. She thought of herself at home in Tullymore on rainy winter nights, coming upstairs after a night in front of the television set, Bernard still shut up in his study, for he never watched telly, and not up to bed yet, for all the difference it made when he did come. She thought of the boredom of home when at night she would think of these holidays in London and Paris and be hungry for the next trip. Those were the nights she would not draw the blinds, but play the innocent, undressing herself before the window, wondering if someone was out there in one of the back gardens of the houses opposite, standing in the rain, staring up at her with his heart in his mouth.

She got into bed. She never wore a nightgown. She put out the light, and as she did a worry came through the champagne haze, the bad worry of this week. But, drowsy with drink, the worry floated out of her mind. In the morning when the champagne had worn off she would be jumpy and sick and sad. But now she felt calm and sated. She slept.

She woke when someone switched on a light in the sitting room. Bernard? But it could be a burglar, you read about nothing but burglars in hotels nowadays. She sat up, looked out into the living room, and saw Bernard wearing his overcoat. She lay down again and shut her eyes, feigning sleep. She sensed that he had come to the bedroom door. All of a sudden she knew that something was very wrong.

"Mona, are you awake?"

"I am now."

"Sorry."

"Are you coming to bed?" It was all she would ask. No questions once you were on holiday. Especially at this hour of the night.

"I'll sleep on the sofa. I've been up all night with Eileen. She's still sick."

She switched on the light. "What's the matter with her?" she asked. Then saw that his eyes were red and sore. He took off his overcoat. He looked as if he had been crying, but she had never in her life seen him cry.

"What's wrong?" she said.

He sat on the edge of the bed. "I've ruined everything."

He eased himself along the edge of the bed, moving toward her. She was surprised. She reached out her arms to him, not sure if she was doing the right thing. He leaned into her embrace and put his face on her naked breasts. "Tell me," she said. "Tell me."

"I'm afraid to tell you."

She looked at the bedside clock. It was ten to three. "Don't be afraid."

"It's something I did behind your back."

"Tell me."

"I've been looking at a house down in Louth. A very big house, much bigger than Tullymore."

A new house? Fear came on her. Was he planning to leave her, was he going to run off with this girl? A divorce, the end of their life together, Tullymore, the shop, holidays, money to burn. After all she had done to make this marriage go, after all she had put up with to accommodate him in his lunatic ways, was this the thanks she got? Anger filled her, but she kept her voice calm. "A house for who?" she asked as Eileen's pale face came before her. Eileen who was his madness, Eileen who had changed him so that he could no longer be trusted, not for a minute.

[83]

"A house for us," he said. "But I thought there'd be a place for Eileen as well. Don't be cross now. I can't stand a row, not tonight. I'm ready to kill myself."

She held him tight then. As long as he was not leaving her, she would help him. "Tell me," she said. "Don't worry, it will be all right."

"Lie down beside me," he said and lay on the bed staring up at the ceiling as she listened to him say that he had done what he swore he would never do. Tell Eileen. And then this whole lunatic secret scheme about buying some bloody mansion down in Louth, without a word to anyone. Oh, God, she had been right to worry that he had gone around the bend. This girl would destroy him. And then he said that Eileen was wanting to go home tomorrow and give up her job in the shop. Which, as she knew, but did not say to him, meant the whole town would know about it within the week.

"Tell me this," she asked him, "did you make a pass at her?"

"Of course not." He sounded offended. "I'd never do a thing like that."

"Did you say anything about us?"

"No."

"You're sure?"

"Of course."

"So that's why she pretended to be taken sick this evening. She didn't want to go out with you after you told her you were in love with her."

"But she was sick," he said. "She vomited. She's very upset. She's such an innocent. Now she wants to leave Lismore and go someplace away from us, away from me. And I'll go after her, I warn you, I'll go after her, no matter where she goes."

"And leave me, is that what you're telling me?"

"I don't want to leave you, but I can't let her go. If I can't be near her, then that's the end of me."

She knew that he meant it. He was not sane anymore. He had changed. He was ready to do anything, but he could do nothing to help himself. She must do it. "Now listen, Bernard," she said. "Nothing has happened. Do you understand? She's still here, she doesn't even have her ticket home. Now, you let me talk to her."

"When? She wants to go in the morning. And what can you say that will change her mind?"

"I'm going to sleep now," Mona McAuley said. "Wake me at eight sharp and have coffee ready. Then I'll go down by myself and talk to her. You're sure she didn't leave tonight?"

"She has no ticket and no money and she was in bed a while ago, when I left her."

"All right. Now, don't you worry your head anymore. I'll speak to her."

"If you can keep her," he said, "I promise you I'll make it up to you."

But she had turned to the wall and composed herself for sleep.

Thursday, August 28

Shortly after seven, Eileen, lying sleepless in bed, saw a morning light appear around the edges of the window blind. She got up and looked out. It was cloudy but not raining. She felt weary and sick, her mind going over and over the events of yesterday and last night. She remembered this was her last morning in London, this city she had wanted so much to see. Suddenly she wanted to go out. Bernard would not ring before eight, so she dressed quickly and, within minutes, was in the lobby moving through a group of American tourists who were waiting for their sightseeing bus. She went out into the chill morning air and turned toward Belgravia, those elegant squares with private parks. At this time of morning the people in these streets were not the rich but cleaning women, postmen, milkmen, and some girls in raincoats and jeans who chatted as they walked in front of her and from their talk seemed to be technicians in a hospital. She envied them. Today she would be back in Lismore, back in a small Irish town where, when you thought of a big city, it was

Belfast. She saw Belfast, saw Donegall Square, the heart of it, the City Hall which had seemed big until this week, saw the British Army armored cars that the people called pigs, going slow down Donegall Street, saw the checkpoint barrier thrown up at a crossroads, the cars and lorries waiting to be searched, saw the bombed back streets, empty as a city in a war. She envied these girls living here among grandeur. To live in London, to have friends your own age, to be able to go out every night, maybe to meet boys who would be different from the ones in Lismore, boys who liked you, boys you liked.

But how could she live here when her mother needed her at home? She saw 19 Church Street, the front sitting room with Mama watching television, Mama who was not expecting her home before Sunday afternoon, Mama who had no notion of what had gone on here, who thought the McAuleys were great. Would her mother believe that Bernard McAuley had been planning to buy a flat in Belfast for her and Aunt Maeve to live in while he took her daughter off to live with him? Would she believe it herself if somebody told it to her? And what if the McAuleys denied everything? And they would. They will.

She saw a clock. It was time to go back to the hotel. Bernard would ring very soon.

It was ten minutes to eight when she walked into the hotel lobby. Each morning she had eaten her breakfast in the lounge. Today, still feeling sick, she would just have a cup of tea. She went into the lounge thinking that, even now, she was ordering things in the expectation that the McAuleys would be paying. There was a new group of Americans in the lounge, including a party of old people, unsuitably dressed, the old men in safari suits, the old ladies like clowns in bright makeup, trousers, and ruffled blouses. All the Americans seemed to carry flight bags as well as plastic duty-free bags filled with liquor and cigarettes, and these littered the floor of the lounge as Eileen looked about for a small table where she could sit alone. In addition to the party of old Americans there were other Americans, some with children, occupying the larger tables and making a great deal of noise. As Eileen went farther into the lounge she saw one small table with a free seat, the other seat being occupied by a girl not much older than herself, a pretty, rather fat blond girl in a checked shirt and blue jeans who was drinking coffee and eating toast. Beside her on the floor was a carryall crib in which there was a lovely little baby, asleep. Eileen went to this table, intending to ask if the empty seat was taken, and as she did the blond girl looked up as though she were expecting her and asked in an American accent, "Are you from Wales?"

"No, I'm from Ireland," Eileen said, and the girl began to laugh.

"I'm sorry," the girl said. "But that's funny. That *is* funny. Excuse me, I'm not laughing at you. You see, I thought you were the baby sitter. I'm expecting a baby sitter from an agency called Wales. I'm sorry."

"Oh, I see," Eileen said. "Excuse me, but is that seat taken?"

"No, no, sit down."

Eileen smiled at the sleeping baby. "What a lovely baby."

"Thank you. I was hoping you'd be our sitter. I'm supposed to meet her here at eight. I hope she shows. My husband and I haven't ever been in London and we're only here till the day after tomorrow, so we want to get out and see things. You know? And this friend of ours who's living in London, he was at school with my husband, he arranged for this sitter, so I'm keeping my fingers crossed. I hope she's not going to be late."

Eileen sat down and looked around for the waiter.

It really was a lovely baby, the sort you'd want to take home with you. And in the way of Americans, the girl went on talking and told how her husband was just out of college and had just got a job with an oil company in the Persian Gulf and how they were off there next week; they had never been to Europe before and this friend of theirs who lived in London had taken them out to dinner last night at the craziest place. And by the time the waiter came and Eileen ordered a cup of tea, she knew that the girl's name was Arlene Simmonds, and that her husband's name was Bill and that they came from some place called Sherman Oaks in California and that Arlene's grandmother came from Ireland and that Arlene would like to visit Ireland someday but that right now the only place she would be seeing besides London was Rome for two days before they reached Kuwait in the Persian Gulf.

"How old is your baby?" Eileen asked when at last there was a lull in Arlene's chat.

"Just five months. She's real good. She slept all the time on the plane. Well, not all the time, but most of it. Oh, say. We passed over Ireland yesterday morning. It looked real pretty. All those little fields and hedges. Sure is green." Arlene looked at her wristwatch, which had a picture of Mickey Mouse on its face. "I wonder what's keeping this sitter. Look, could I ask you to stay here with the baby while I go call this friend of ours who's supposed to have made the arrangements?"

"Yes, all right," Eileen said, and Arlene got up, took her purse, and went out to the lobby, leaving her baby with a total stranger. Eileen watched Arlene hurry off among the tables. If I had a little baby like this I'd be terrified of letting it out of my sight. But, then, Americans seemed to trust everybody and to talk to everybody. The Persian Gulf. Eileen could not remember

exactly where that was, it was one of those desert king-
doms in the Middle East. She thought of Arlene, a girl
about her own age, but married and with a baby, flying
halfway across the world to a place she had never been,
passing through London and Rome to live in a house in
the Persian Gulf. She looked down at the sleeping baby,
then pulled the crib closer until the baby lay at her
feet. Imagine having a baby. Having it at your breast.

And just then she looked up, looked across the
crowded lounge in the direction Arlene had gone, and
saw, coming in from the lobby, Mona McAuley, wearing
a smart roll-neck beige sweater and a beige skirt. Mona
seemed worried. She was looking for someone, and when
her head turned in Eileen's direction, there came on
her face such a smile of relief. She hurried at once
toward Eileen, passing through the groups of tourists,
saying as she came up, "Well, thank God, I've been
looking for you everywhere. Were you out or something?"

"I went for a bit of a walk. I didn't think you people
would be up yet."

"A walk?" Mona sat down in Arlene's seat. "I should
walk more myself. I remember the first time I came to
London, I walked all over the place." And then, suddenly, Mona saw the baby carrier. "Whose is that?" she
asked, astonished.

"It belongs to an American girl," Eileen said. "She
asked me to keep an eye on it while she makes a phone
call. She's waiting for a baby sitter."

Mona looked into the crib again. "It can't be more
than two months old," she said. "Although I know
nothing about babies. Aren't Americans the end,
though? Imagine leaving your baby with a perfect
stranger." She looked at Eileen, smiling, shaking her
head, marveling. Eileen looked down at the baby, for

she found it hard to hear Mona talking about strangers without seeing the Mona of last night, sitting in this very lounge, smiling a smile like a net to trap strange men. "Anyway," Mona said. "I have to talk to you. It's about something quite serious. Will she be long, this girl?"

"I don't think so."

"Have you had your breakfast yet?"

"I just had tea."

"Are you still feeling sick?"

Eileen shook her head. "Good," Mona said. "Well, maybe we could go up to your room. It would be quieter there, if that's all right."

"All right. Do you know that I'm going home today?"

"I know. That's what I want to talk to you about."

How much had Bernard told her, Eileen wondered, had he told her about the house in County Louth, or will I have to be the one to tell her that? Suddenly she wished that she could be sick, so sick she would have to be sent home on a stretcher, not well enough to talk to anyone. And then she saw Arlene come back into the lounge, smiling as she approached. "Hi, there," Arlene said. She looked at Mona, who rose, saying, "I have your seat. I'm sorry."

"No, that's okay."

"Did you get the sitter?" Eileen asked.

"No. I was trying to reach Earl, this friend of Bill's I told you about. All I got is his answering service. Anyway"—Arlene bent down and picked up the baby's carryall crib—"I'd better go upstairs and talk to my husband. Thanks a lot for looking after Maudie." She smiled at them both. "Nice meeting you."

And then, as they were all leaving the lounge together, Mona put her hand on Eileen's arm, detaining her, letting the American girl go ahead. "Wait," Mona said. "I have an idea. There's a writing room just off the dining room. Nobody ever uses it. Why don't we go in there?"

The writing room was a small, dark, rectangular room with escritoire desks lined up in a row as in a school-room. At the far end of the room, by the window, were two Louis XV armchairs and a small end table. "All right here?" Mona asked, pointing to these chairs. They sat, facing the window which looked out on the Garden Court. Mona glanced back toward the doorway as though to make sure no one could overhear, then began to speak in a low, anxious voice. "First of all, I'm very sorry this has happened. I was afraid of something like this, if you came to London."

"You didn't want me to come?"

"No. You see, I've known for some time how Bernard feels about you. I know he never said anything to you. I believed he never would. Of course, I didn't know about this latest madness of his, buying a house in Louth, and all that."

"But if you knew he felt that way, why didn't you do something about it? And why did you let him bring me to London? I don't understand."

"Look, it's not that simple," Mona said. "I don't understand Bernard myself. I'm beginning to wonder if he's a well man." She stared at Eileen as she said this, as though to impress the seriousness of this state-ment on her. In the cold early light from the window, Eileen saw that Mona, who had taken professional courses at Elizabeth Arden, was made up wrongly this morning: all of the colors intensified, as though she had used evening instead of daytime makeup.

"But what's wrong with him?" Eileen asked.

"I don't know. I think"—and Mona paused, as though gathering her reins for a great leap—"I think he might be having a nervous breakdown."

Eileen sat, silent. She thought of him last night in the

wine bar, crying, talking in that wild way. "Yes," she said. "Yes, I suppose you could be right."

"I don't know," Mona said. "I mean, I have nothing to go on, for he'd never see a doctor. But he was supposed to have had some sort of breakdown years ago. It was his cousin Sean Doyle, do you know him, who told me. He said Bernard's father hushed it up. But it was the time Bernard came home from the monastery."

"The monastery?" Eileen said.

"Didn't you know about that?"

"I remember him telling me that while he was at Queen's he decided to change over and study for the priesthood, but that his father talked him out of it. Something about giving him a new car."

"That's how he tells it," Mona said. "As a sort of joke. But he was dead serious at the time. He left Queen's in his second year and he actually went into a Benedictine monastery in Cavan as a lay brother."

"Bernard did?"

"Word of honor. He was in there for about six months, and then he came back home and finished his degree and went into the business. But Sean says that when he came home he had a sort of nervous breakdown for a while. He's very intense, you know."

"I know."

"And I've never seen him as intense as he is now, with this business about you. He's not himself. So I just wonder. It could be a breakdown."

"But couldn't you get a doctor to talk to him? Isn't there somebody who could help him?"

"Nobody can help Bernard except you and me. Anyway, if I told a doctor that Bernard wasn't himself, Bernard would laugh at me and the doctor would believe him, not me. Sure, you know, he can charm the birds out of the trees. Nobody knows what sort of man he is. Nobody knows how difficult he is. It's me people think is the difficult one," Mona said, her voice suddenly becoming angry. "I know there're people at home who say we don't have children because I'm too vain about my figure. I'll bet you heard that one."

"No, I haven't," Eileen said. "I never heard anybody say things about either of you."

"Then you don't hear much," Mona said. "There are a whole lot of people who are jealous of me. You'd think I set out to catch Bernard, when it was the other way around. I had plenty of other offers, you know. Plenty."

"I know. That's why I don't understand all this."

"How could anybody understand Bernard when he doesn't understand himself?" Mona said. "All I know is, he chased after me, wanting me to marry him. And he's used to getting what he wants. But once he gets something he doesn't know if he wants it anymore. Oh, I don't know. I'll never know him. Look at the way he went behind my back, arranging for you to come to London."

"I didn't know he did that. Honestly, Mona, if I'd known, I never would have come. After all, you lent me a dress to come. How was I to know you didn't want me?"

"How could I explain to you?" Mona said. "He would have killed me."

"Well, anyway," Eileen said. She felt herself red in the face with embarrassment. "I think the best thing I can do now is go home and hope he'll just leave me alone."

"I believe you're talking of giving up your job with us. That's what you told Bernard, isn't it?"

"I think it's the only thing."

"It's not the only thing," Mona said. "In fact, it would

be the worst thing you could do at this stage. Now look, will you help me?"

"I don't know. I suppose it depends."

"All right. First of all, there's no need for you to run off home today. That will solve nothing; it will just mean he'll be on the next plane after you. So why don't you please stay and finish the holiday with us?"

"With us. With Bernard, you mean."

"All right, fair enough, it was my fault going off and leaving you alone with him so much. But it won't be like that from now on. Who knows, we might even enjoy ourselves?"

"How could we?"

"Well, all right," Mona said and smiled. "But Bernard will enjoy it." Her smile was knowing and complicit, and at that moment Eileen felt she had at last seen the real Mona McAuley, not the business Mona who ran the shop, not the Mona who gave great parties at home, not the Mona other women envied for her looks and her figure, not even the hypocrite Mona who, away from home, lured men up to her room. The real Mona was this one: the Mona who was not going to let anything or anyone ruin her marriage, the Mona who had sold herself and now was asking Eileen to sell herself as well.

"Besides," Mona said, "it's only three more days. And it would save a lot of explanations to your mother, and so on."

Eileen did not speak.

"Do you know what I think?" Mona said. "I think it would be nice if you would do that for me, after all I've done for you."

Of course she would say that, it was what Eileen had been waiting for her to say, waiting for it and dreading it. She was unable to look Mona in the eye. "I'm sorry," she mumbled. She heard Mona take a breath as if about to say something sharp, but instead Mona leaned over and put her hand on Eileen's knee.

"Eileen, listen, when I gave you the job I had no notion that any of this would happen. Frankly, I couldn't believe it when Bernard told me. So I don't want you to think I was in cahoots with him."

"I don't."

"So do me a favor, please. Don't go home today. Think of your mother. You know what a worry it is to her to think you have to support her. And then, if you tell her, you'll have to find a new job. And jobs are not easy nowadays. Honestly, I have dozens of people coming in all the time with qualifications as good or better than yours. Listen, I'm not asking you to do anything wrong. I don't think you understand. I'm saying that if you'll just forget any of this happened, neither Bernard nor I will ever say one word to you about it again."

"But how can you say that when you just said that Bernard's not well and you don't know what he might do?"

"I never said that. I know very well what he'll do if I go upstairs now and tell him I've patched it up with you. He'll never speak of it to you again. Don't you see, he'll do anything to keep you from disappearing. And after a while, who knows, he'll probably get over this notion of his. If you help and if I help. Please, Eileen?"

"I don't know," Eileen said. She felt like crying. "I just don't think I should stay on."

"I'll tell you what you'll do," Mona said. "Just go upstairs to your room now and think about what I've said. Remember, I've told you all this in confidence. Nobody's forcing you. If your answer is still that you can't help me, say, an hour from now, I'll tell Bernard your decision and we'll take you to the airport. God knows what will happen after that. But it's up to you. All right?"

Eileen nodded and stood up. It was like long ago in convent school at the end of a talk with Reverend Mother. Nothing had been solved or settled, but the moment the talk was over it seemed as if it had. Getting away was the settlement. She preceded Mona out of the writing room and walked blunderingly through the crowded lobby, hoping Mona would not follow her to the lift. At the lift she looked back and saw that Mona had gone to the house telephone. When the lift came Eileen got in, in a crush of American tourists. When she got to her room she locked the door and began to pack.

Bernard sat at the table in the sitting room of the McAuleys' suite. He wore the gray pinstripe suit he had worn on the first day of his London visit. On the chair beside him lay a raincoat and a pair of brown suede gloves. Breakfast coffee had been trundled in on a serving table and stood, untasted, a little to his left. In front of him he had placed his thin gold wristwatch. He sat, completely immobile, with his hands pressed flat-palmed against the table as though to prevent their trembling. He stared straight ahead. He had sat in this position ever since Mona came back up and told him the news. Now, as she came from the bathroom and lingered in the doorway of the sitting room, he gave no indication that he knew he was no longer alone. She knew he was waiting for the hour to pass. She did not know what he was thinking. He was no longer pleading or dependent as he had been last night. She knew she would be judged by results.

The telephone rang. She saw him jerk his head up just perceptibly, as though by a great effort of will he restrained himself from answering it.

"I'll get it," she said and went to the phone, which was on a side table by the window. It could be the hotel, it could be a business call from Ireland, it could be Eileen. She did not think it was Eileen. After all, it was only about twenty minutes since she had left Eileen in the lobby.

But it was.

"Mona?"

"Yes, Eileen."

"Mona, I've packed. I'm sorry, but I think I'd like to go home today."

"Oh, my God," Mona said. To think this little bitch was dictating to her after all she'd done for her. To think she was getting away with it.

"I'm sorry," the little bitch said again.

"Oh, you're not sorry," Mona said in a rage. "You're downright selfish, so you are. You don't give a damn about anybody but yourself."

Something hit Mona hard on the back of her neck, knocking her forward. As she stumbled, Bernard wrenched the receiver away from her. She stood, gasping, feeling the pain of the blow. He had struck her with his fist, Bernard, who had never hit her in his life.

"Hello," he said into the phone. "Eileen? It's Bernard. You want to go, then?" He listened, then said, "No, no, that's all right, it's quite all right. And listen, I don't agree with Mona at all. I apologize for what she said." He listened. "No, no, I'll take you out to the airport. No, I insist. We'll see what we can do. Let's think. The first flight I have you wait-listed on is at half-eleven. It's about half-nine now. Well, we should leave here at ten to be on the safe side. That all right? Ten. Okay, I'll meet you downstairs in the lobby at ten. Good."

He put the receiver down.

"Have you gone mad?" Mona said.

"It's you who's gone mad." He turned and went into the bathroom and shut the door.

"Why is it me who's gone mad?" she shouted through the door. "Punching me! Listen, I did everything I could. It's not my fault if that wee bitch has made a lunatic out of you." She went to the mirror and craned to see if the blow had left a mark on her neck. There was no mark. "What are you going to do, then?" she shouted. "Are you going to let her go home and tell her mother that you're in love with her? Punching *me*. You're the one that's ruined everything, bringing her here behind my back and spilling your guts out to her. What's going to happen when that gets talked about at home, what are you going to do, deny it? Or run after her again and let the whole town know about it? In love, *you in love*, what a joke."

She heard him run water in the washbasin. She had gone too far. She could imagine him standing in there, listening, his narrow face cold, drying his hands, getting ready to take Eileen to the airport. And as she was thinking of that, the bathroom door opened and he came out. Cold: his face shut to her. "Is there a back entrance, or back stairs or any other way a guest could go out of here without going through the lobby?" he asked her. He spoke as if she were some hotel maid.

"No, not that I know of. Why?"

"She might try to dodge out." He went past her and put on his raincoat, slipping the suede gloves in his pocket.

"Bernard, I'm sorry," she said. "It was just that you hit me."

"I'll go down and sit in the lobby. If she rings here, tell her I'm waiting for her downstairs."

"I said I was sorry."

"I'm not interested in your sorrow."

"Do you think she'll get a flight home today?"

He looked at her as though she had said something irrelevant and irritating. Then he went to the door. "Wait," she said. "What do you want me to do? Do you want to meet me here later?"

He stopped, his back to her. "Do what you want," he said. "I don't want to see you." He opened the door, then paused. He did not look back at her. "Oh," he said. "One thing. I don't want to come back and find somebody in this suite."

"Don't worry."

He shut the door and was gone.

Eileen wore her raincoat and packed her umbrella so as to make it easier to carry her own suitcase. When she came downstairs into the lobby with her case, she saw Bernard sitting incongruously beside two bellboys on the porters' bench by the front door of the hotel. She knew he had chosen to sit there so as not to miss her. When he saw her he got up and hurried toward her, at the same time signaling a porter to follow him. "Take the lady's suitcase," he ordered the porter. "And wait for us outside."

"I can manage it," she said ineffectually, but let the porter take her case away. Bernard smiled at her. "Ready, then?" he asked.

"Yes."

"I told the hall porter to line up a taxi. I knew you wouldn't want to be waiting around."

As he spoke he led her across the lobby to the hall porter's desk, where one of the hall porters, the short one, hurried out, going ahead of them toward the front door, saying: "I have the taxi for you, Mr. McAuley."

And then they were outside, the porter with her bag going down the front steps ahead of them, the hall porter pointing out the taxi he had taken from the rank and made to park across the street, the doorman blowing his whistle for the taxi to circle around and come to them, then the three men in livery, bowing as Bernard brought out tips, their respectful, cheerful voices, saying: "Thank you, sir. Thank you. Have a good journey, miss. Where to, sir?" and the doorman opening the taxi door for them and repeating Bernard's order to the taxi man. "Heath-row. Terminal One." The door shut, the big London taxi eased out from the curb, it's driver sealed off behind his glass panel, and it was over; she was like Cinderella coming home from the ball at midnight, this was the end of that attention, the end of the McAuleys' money, the end of London. For now that she was in the taxi with Bernard and he was being nice, not angry and nasty like Mona, she knew that he would get her on a plane today. That was what he was good at, getting things done. She looked at him. He had turned up his raincoat collar as though to hide his face and sat looking out of the taxi window as if interested in the swift-passing streets. "This is very nice of you," she said.

"It's all right," he said. "You don't have to talk." He laughed. "It's a long ride out to the airport. Especially when you're with someone you don't want to be with."

"I mean it," she said. "It is nice of you."

He nodded and kept on looking out the window. Had he really been a monk in a monastery? She thought of the monks she used to see in Dublin, walking along the Liffey, sometimes with shopping bags, wearing long, brown woolen robes and funny open sandals. To think of Bernard, who cared so much about his clothes, got up in a long, brown robe like a woman's dress with his bare big toe sticking out of a sandal. And yet it was not hard to see him as a religious person. She could see him in front of a tabernacle praying all night in some religious vigil. She could see him staring at the altar, his dark eyes intense.

They sat in silence. The taxi was out on some sort of motorway now, moving at top speed. Bernard did not look at her and she was grateful, if embarrassed, by his silence. At last, when they had come off the motorway and were on what seemed to be a highway leading to the airport, he asked. "Did you give your mother a ring, by any chance?"

"No, why?"

"I don't know. I thought you might have wanted to tell her you were on your way home."

"I thought I'd ring her when I got to Belfast. There'll be plenty of time while I'm waiting for a bus."

"You'll not take a bus," he said. "You'll take a taxi."

"I will not. A taxi all the way to Lismore?"

"I'll give you a number to ring in Belfast and you'll charge it to my account. Now, don't argue with me. It's the least I can do."

She thought: I'll not argue, I'll just take the bus.

And in that moment money came into her head, as it had earlier that morning when she was lying in bed. She had nothing saved, her mother hadn't either. She would get unemployment until she could find some other job. They would manage. But managing was all they had ever been able to do, managing meant going without most things you wanted, it meant that every-thing must be planned and saved for. People like Ber-nard had never known that sort of scrimping and saving. I suppose that's part of it, she decided. I suppose it's hard for me to feel sorry for anybody as rich as he is.

"By the way," he said, "you won't have to go back into the shop. We'll just say you're giving your notice now and I'll keep you on full salary for three months. That way, you'll have time to look around for something that suits you."

She was startled: it was as though he had read her thoughts. "There's no need," she said. "Isn't two weeks the usual notice?"

"There's no usual." He was still looking out the window. "You've been with us for over a year and your leaving isn't your fault, it's mine. So three months is only fair."

She did not answer. She did not want to be always saying thank you. He was right that it was his fault that she was leaving. She hadn't thought of that. And so they drove on in silence, beginning to move among thick traffic on an approach road to the airport. Suddenly the sky gonged with the sound of planes. She wondered about the weather. It was only her second time to fly. "It looks very cloudy," she said.

He squinted up through the window. "It's overcast, but not enough to stop flights. This isn't my lucky day, is it?"

And now they came to the terminal itself, the taxi drawing up in a bustle of arriving people, car doors slamming, suitcases multiplying on the pavement. Bernard jumped out, signaling to a porter, the taxi driver very pleased, saying, "Thanks very much, guv," when Bernard paid him, and the porter and Bernard walking ahead, Bernard explaining to the porter not to check in her suitcase yet because she was on standby, and then they all three went up on a moving staircase to the big terminal waiting hall, where Bernard stationed her on a seat in the middle of the hall while he and the porter went off to join a line at the British Airways counter. At the end of the room a huge board listed flights to different cities. It was strange to see Belfast up there among faraway places. But everything seemed far away when you were here in London, in this great city of monuments and palaces and big shops and wide streets. There was so much money here, there were so many more rich people than she had ever seen at home. Even Bernard seemed richer here than he did at home, for at home, while he had the best of everything, even his Mercedes looked more ordinary in High Street than it would in front of Harrods, and at home, even though he was always well dressed, she would sometimes see him coming off a building site with contractors, or coming out of one of his pubs with his managers, and he would look quite ordinary. Was it coming to England so often that had given him the notion of wanting to be the lord of some house with stables and a ballroom? She looked over at him now as he stood in line with the porter; with his raincoat and his pinstripe suit and gloves, he looked gentlemanly and rich, the sort of man who should not have to wait in a queue. She watched him reach the counter and talk to the clerk behind the desk. Then he said something to the porter and he and the porter left the counter and came back in her direction. The porter put the suitcase down by her seat and said, "Thanks very much indeed, sir," when Bernard tipped him. The porter went off. Bernard sat down beside her. "Doesn't look very promising. There are six people wait-listed before you. Would you like a cup of tea?"

She said no, but he got up and went off and brought back two mugs of tea. "We have to wait, anyway," he explained, and sat beside her, leaning forward, holding the mug of tea in front of him, like a beggar with a begging bowl. She sat, feeling the special nervousness of not knowing if she was going or staying. She thought of asking him to give her her ticket and leave her here alone because this might take hours and hours. But looking at him, sitting there with his untasted tea, she knew there was nowhere else he wanted to be. She began to watch the big notice board. Every few minutes the information would change on the arrival or departure of flights. The change occurred with a sudden shuffling noise as the black counters flipped over and new numerals came up. The flight to Belfast shuffled. A gate had now been assigned. And the flight was listed as ON TIME.

Bernard seemed to remember something. He put down his tea, took out his little gold-edged lizard notebook, wrote in it with a thin pencil, then tore out a sheet and handed it to her. "This is the telephone number you call in Belfast to get a taxi to Lismore. And the number below that is my account number with the firm. Just give the number and they'll charge it, tip and all."

She thanked him and put the sheet in her purse. Maybe, if she couldn't get a bus. After all, as he had said, it was his fault, this mess.

"Oh, that reminds me," he said. "I had planned quite an evening for us tomorrow night. It was supposed to be your last night in London, and after the theater you and I were to go on to supper at Le Gavroche and meet Mona there if she was free. Le Gavroche is supposed to be *the* place in London now. Full of film stars and what have you."

"Maybe you can persuade Mona to go to the theater first," she said, but he seemed not to hear. He put away his little notebook. "And the show tomorrow night isn't a play, it's a musical. I thought you might like that for a change. I'm not keen on musicals myself, but this one is all the rage. It was a big hit on Broadway, whatever that means." He smiled. "I was in America once."

"I didn't know that."

"Yes, when I was a little boy. I have an aunt living there, she has quite a bit of money, she invited me over after my mother died. She lives in Brookline, Massachusetts. Not exactly the Paris of the Western world. Still, she met me in New York and we spent a few days there first. I remember the Plaza Hotel and a gorilla in the Central Park Zoo. And the skyscrapers. But I suppose I remember that trip mostly because I learned something about the power of money. I didn't like my aunt much but I liked the great time she gave me." He smiled and looked at Eileen. "You see, not all of us have your moral fortitude."

"I don't have moral fortitude."

"Oh, yes, you do. Or you think you do. I suppose I should say I admire that, but I don't. You're just another example of a wee girl who is taught, 'This is right and that is wrong,' and who believes it without thinking, simply because some priest says it's so. Or the nuns. The nuns in Ballycastle. That's where you went to school, wasn't it? Ballycastle convent."

"Yes, Ballycastle." She wanted to say, and you, what about you, you must have believed it once if you wanted to go off and become a monk. But it was better not to: be quiet and hope to get on the plane. She looked again at the notice board and saw the shuffling beginning. The information was changing beside DUBLIN. "Look," she said. "Do you see that? There's a flight from Dublin that's delayed."

"Where, where?" He stood up, peered shortsightedly, then went a few steps closer to the board. "So it is." He turned and looked at her. "Wait here a minute," he said and set off in his long, half-running stride. She watched him talking to a clerk at the Aer Lingus counter, watched until he turned and came back to her. "Apparently Dublin's socked in," he said. "Thick fog and they're not expecting a let-up, so the plane can't get out. The one you were wait-listed on hasn't even left Dublin."

"What do you think, then?"

"I think unless you get on this next flight to Belfast we might as well turn around and go back to London and try again tomorrow. You're not wait-listed on any other flights, and both airlines say they have long waiting lists for every other flight today."

"Maybe, if you just gave me my ticket and left me here? There's no need for you to hang about all day."

"No, no. Look, you'll just have to believe one thing: I'm trying to help you get out. If I say there are no more chances of getting out today, that's the truth. Go on up there and ask them if you don't believe me." He pointed to the Aer Lingus counter and she could see he was worked up into a temper. "Do you think I'm lying?" he said in a loud voice, so that the people on the bench next to hers looked up at him as if he was someone who would make a scene.

"No, no, of course not," she told him. "No, Bernard, please. Come and sit down."

"No," he said. "Look, I'm doing all I can. Now, just stay there and I'll go and make some more inquiries. I know it's a terrible imposition for you to have to put up with my company for another day. Believe me, I'd move heaven and earth to get you home if I could. I know the sight of me makes you sick."

And rushed off, she watching as he headed back to the British Airways counter and talked to a clerk there, then half ran over to the Aer Lingus counter. She supposed he really *was* trying. After all, if she went back to London with him now she didn't have to go out with him tonight, she could just stay in the hotel and try for a flight again tomorrow. And if the absolute worst happened, she had her flight booked on Sunday, it was only two days off. But two days seemed an eternity. He was coming back. He sat down beside her and said, "I'm sorry. It seems I can't work miracles."

"I'm the one who should say I'm sorry. And I am sorry, Bernard. I know I'm being a pain in the neck. If there's no room on this Belfast plane, let's go back to London. At least, that way, your whole day won't be spoiled."

"That's the girl," he said. "That's sensible." He looked at his watch. "We'll know in less than an hour. In the meantime, I'm going to stretch my legs. All right?"

"Of course." She guessed he was being tactful, going off like that. She sat and watched the board. After a while the Belfast flight was announced. He came back and told her he was keeping in touch. There were no no-shows yet, he said.

"What are no-shows?"

"People who book but don't show up." He looked at the board. "We have to wait until the last minute in case they do. They hold the seats until the people are boarding the plane."

"I see," she said. She sat and waited, and at last there was an announcement of final call for passengers to Belfast. A little red light began flashing on and off the board beside the Belfast flight. Bernard went over to the counter. He came back to her.

"No luck," he said. "They're full up."

It felt expected. Somehow, she had known it would not be that easy. She stood up. "All right, then," she said. "Will we try tomorrow?"

The porter summoned by Bernard to carry Eileen's suitcase led the way as they went back down to the ground-floor level. "Are you going into central London, sir?" the porter asked.

[109]

"Yes."

"I'm afraid there's a bit of a queue for taxis. Very busy, today."

"How long a wait?" Bernard asked.

"Depends, sir. Twenty minutes, half an hour."

Now, as they came out into the departure area, Eileen saw that the porter was right, there was a very long queue winding around and around, people with luggage, dispatchers whistling, taxis moving up. Some of the people, Indians and other foreigners, not understanding the obedient British, kept trying to jump the queue. The porter led on toward the end of the line, but as they moved through the crowds of people coming out of the terminal, Bernard stopped and waved and Eileen saw a big man waving back, a man with a red complexion, wearing a tweed suit with brown-and-white checks and a black woolen shirt with a red wool tie, a man so tall he stuck up over the other people around him, calling out, "Bernard! Hello there," in a loud English-sounding voice. And yet as Bernard went to him, she knew the man was not English, there was something Irish about his face and complexion: he was the sort of Protestant you would see at the Horse Show in Dublin, and as though confirming her notion, he turned to the woman beside him, a stout, jolly-looking woman in a riding mac and a tweed skirt. And then all three turned to Eileen, with Bernard saying: "This is Eileen Hughes, she's a friend of ours, she was trying to get home today, but no luck." And they said "How do you do" in accents that were English but not quite. They were probably well-to-do Irish Prods. And when Bernard said their names, she was sure of it. "This is Betty and Derek Irwin." And both shook hands with her warmly. They were obviously great friends of Bernard's, for they now said: "How long have you been in London,

Bernard? You never told us. Do you mean we wouldn't have seen you?" But Bernard said of course they would, he had been meaning to call them. And then asked what they were doing at the airport. It seemed that Derek had come to pick up his wife, who had just come in on the flight from Belfast, and he said he had his car here and offered them a lift back to town. "Will that be all right?" Bernard asked her in a whisper, so that the Irwins did not hear. And she nodded yes, because of course it was all right, it meant she would not have to drive back alone with him.

So she and Betty Irwin waited outside the terminal doors, having the usual conversation about the weather, while Derek and Bernard went off to get Derek's car, which turned out to be a large battered estate car, with hockey sticks and a skateboard in the back. As they started off out of the airport, Derek asked if they had had lunch and Bernard said not yet and Derek said: "Look, why don't you both come back to the house and join us for a late lunch. Maybe the kids will still be around. And what about Mona, could she join us?"

"Mona's out shopping," Bernard said. "I'd not know how to reach her." And then, uncertainly, to Eileen: "What do you think?"

"Oh, do come," Betty said. "We'd love to have you, and the kids will be thrilled. Bernard's my son's godfather."

"Mammonfather is more like it," Derek said and slewed around in the driver's seat, turning his rather handsome purplish face full tilt at Eileen. "You have the deciding vote, it seems."

"Well, I don't mind, it's up to Bernard, really. I mean, thanks very much, if it's not too much trouble." Raging at herself for the awkward way she put it, like a servant, but she couldn't help it, they were older than she and she was always uneasy with the likes of them, English accents, Protestants, money.

"Well, then, we'd love to come," Bernard said.

"Then, that's settled," Betty said. Derek and Bernard began to talk about the Ireland-English rugby match, and as the talk went on, Eileen gathered that Derek was a doctor with a practice in Hampstead and that he had been at Queen's with Bernard and that, later, he and Betty had bumped into Bernard and Mona unexpectedly once during a holiday in Venice. "That was the time we lost her, the second night," Derek said. "Remember that? She went for a walk and got lost and walked around for hours and hours trying to find her way back to the hotel."

"Oh, she's always doing things like that," Bernard said. "Disappearing." But when he said it Eileen noticed that Betty Irwin looked a wee bit skeptical. Then turned to Eileen and asked, "And do you live in Lismore?"

"Eileen is Mona's right hand at the big shop," Bernard said. "And we're great friends." He twisted around in the front seat and looked back at Eileen. "We're still friends, aren't we?" he asked, smiling, but with that strange frightened look in his dark eyes.

"Of course," she said, wanting to kill him.

"I promised to get her on the plane today," Bernard said to the Irwins. "And I failed in my promise."

"Oh, the planes are impossible at this time of year," Betty Irwin said, but Eileen saw her glance at Bernard as though she had noticed his peculiar look. And then Derek asked Bernard about some scandal in the Dublin government and the talk went away from Eileen as Derek piloted them into London and up to Hampstead, which Eileen recognized as the place she had been in on the day they went to Kenwood House. Derek drove along the edge of Regent's Park and turned into an avenue of Victorian villas. The Irwins' was the corner house, the biggest one on the avenue, with a pretty and untidy garden hidden from the street by high stone walls. It was the sort of house Eileen would have loved to live in, and now as she followed Betty Irwin up the front steps and into a hall with a big living room off to the left, she felt at home at once, for while all of the furniture was very good, armchairs and tables and carpets had a used look, a feeling of a family living there in a relaxed informal way. There were walls of books, and the paintings seemed to have been chosen by the Irwins, not handed down through family. To live in London and live here. She thought of her mother's house in Church Street. She wouldn't like the Irwins to know she lived in a wee house like that.

"Drink?" Derek was saying and they all went down to a room in the basement part of the house, a room which looked out on the garden. Gin-and-tonics were poured and a glass of wine for Eileen and for the young baby sitter, who now came in with the children: a boy of six, who was introduced as Christopher, and a four-year-old girl, who was Melissa. Watching Bernard swing Christopher up over his head, Eileen thought of him coming here sometimes when he was alone in London and Mona off someplace. She thought of the skeptical look on Betty's face when Derek said that, about Mona getting lost in Venice. And as Derek and Bernard started talking to each other about the books they were reading, she realized their friendship was the sort Bernard did not have in Lismore, where he had no friends with his interests in painting and architecture and books. While the men talked she and Betty went to the kitchen to get the lunch, which was good food with no fuss, a big salad, cold ham, brown bread, radishes, cheese, and a thick vegetable soup. And more wine. The children had already eaten and now the baby sitter took them upstairs while the grownups sat down to table. The Irwins told a funny story about a man they and Bernard had known at Queen's, telling it for Eileen to make her laugh. And she did laugh. The sick feeling she had had since yesterday disappeared, and she realized that Derek did not have his red face for nothing, for he was a heavy hand with the drink, which he kept on the floor under the table and would bring up often to make sure all glasses were filled. She noticed, too, that Bernard still kept an eye on her, as though afraid she might get up and leave. He kept bringing her into the conversation, saying, "Derek, tell Eileen about the time our boat capsized in Portstewart," or asking her opinion of the actors in the play they had seen the other night. And then, after Betty served coffee, Bernard and Derek went up to Derek's study to look at some book, while Eileen and Betty cleared the dishes into the kitchen. They began to wash up, Betty washing and Eileen drying. "You know," Betty said, "Bernard's always talking about you. I was beginning to wonder if we'd ever meet you."

"Talking about *me?*"

"Well, I don't think he's aware of it, but the last time we bumped into him in Belfast and went for a drink, he and Mona had just been to Dublin with you. And he just talked and talked about you. It's obvious he's very fond of you."

"Oh, they've both been very good to me," Eileen said. She felt she was being cross-examined. "It was Mona who gave me the job. She's been great. It was when my mother got ill and couldn't work and I had to get a job."

"And how is she, your mother? Bernard said something now in the car about you going home because she was ill."

"Oh, did he? Well, yes, I'm worried about her being alone. I'll be glad to get back."

[114]

"Yes, I imagine," Betty said and handed Eileen a colander to dry. "How long have you known the McAuleys, then? About a year?"

"A little longer than that," Eileen said.

Betty laughed, a jolly, fat-woman laugh. "I'm terrible," she said. "Quizzing you like this. It's frightfully rude of me. But I don't know. Bernard just seems a different man since he met you."

Dully, Eileen took up the soup tureen and began to dry it. The sick feeling was back, made worse by the heaviness of the wine.

"Oh, dear," Betty was saying. "I'm sorry. I've put my foot in it. I didn't mean to upset you. Please. Look, we're awfully fond of Bernard, both of us. I mean, Bernard is the one we care about in that marriage. I just don't think, somehow, that he has an easy time of it. And now, seeing you with him today and liking you so much and seeing the way he looks at you. It's just that I hate pretense. So I thought I'd ask. Please forgive me. I'm sorry."

"No, it's all right. But there's nothing at all. Nothing. I work for them, that's all."

"Of course," Betty said. She wiped her hands on a towel and handed Eileen a second clean towel. "Look, let's leave the rest of this and go find the men. We'll talk about something else, shall we?"

"It's all right, really. Don't worry about it." She said it and tried to smile as she said it, so as not to let Betty think she was annoyed. She followed Betty upstairs into the big sitting room, which opened into another room with a desk in it. Bernard and Derek were at the desk looking at a book of photographs, and when Bernard saw Eileen come in, he came forward at once. "All right?" he asked her in a confidential voice. "We meant to join you sooner."

"Yes, fine," she said. She saw that Betty had gone to

the other end of the room. "Actually," she said, in a whisper, "I think I'd like to leave now. I'd like to walk for a bit. You stay."

"No, I'll come with you. We could walk back part of the way through Regent's Park."

He turned to Derek and Betty. "I think we're going to walk part of the way back. Good for us."

"Exercise," Derek said. "As a doctor, I can tell you it's very overrated. Why don't we open some Moselle and sit in the garden. This is my half day."

But Bernard knew she had had enough and he was the one who managed things, thanking Betty and Derek, but all the same getting them out. It was as if he guessed that something had gone wrong. He asked Derek about some pills he needed and Derek wrote him a prescription, and then there were handshakes and smiles all around and promises to see each other again, and they went down through the garden and were in the street, when she remembered her suitcase.

"My case," she said. "I left it in your car."

"So you did," Derek said. "I'll fetch it. But what about your walk? Tell you what. I have to pop down to Chelsea later on this afternoon, I'll drop it off at your hotel." He turned to Bernard. "The Garden Court, is it?"

"Yes," Bernard said. "That would be perfect. Just leave it with the hall porter."

"But that would be too much trouble for you," Eileen said, embarrassed, and worried too, for she would never think of leaving her suitcase to be driven around London and handed over to hall porters. "No, let me take it now," she said, but Bernard said: "Why? No need." And as Derek and Betty seemed to think this settled it, she thanked them again and they said goodbye and shut the garden gate, and there she was in the avenue with Bernard, alone again, the two of them.

"How was that?" he asked. "Was it a terrible bore for you?"

"No, no, they're very nice."

"I had a feeling when you came upstairs just now that Betty had said something to you."

"What would she say to me?"

"Well, I was worried quite a few times during lunch. Because, to tell you the truth, the last time I met them I remember singing your praises. Very indiscreet, I know, but Derek has a habit of giving you one drink too many. And Betty's very sharp, she misses nothing. I wondered if she'd caught on."

"Caught on to what?" Eileen had begun to walk very fast along the avenue and he had to change his stride to catch up.

"Caught on about the way I feel about you."

"I thought we weren't going to talk about that anymore."

"Sorry," he said. "By the way, if we go down there, past the zoo, we can go into the park and walk a good bit of the way."

"I'd rather you'd let me go for a walk alone."

"Oh. Oh, sorry. But let me show you the way. Do you have money in case you need a taxi?"

"Yes."

He walked with her past iron railings and a sign which said LONDON ZOO. Big double-decker buses went past and joggers came by them on the pavement, sweating, breathing in heavy animal grunts. After about three hundred yards they reached a park gate. "Go in here," Bernard said. "Continue on straight and you'll come to the lower end of the park. Keep going, always straight, and you'll come out at Portland Place. You can get a taxi from there. I'll see you at the hotel, then. And in the meantime, I'll look into your chances of getting a flight tomorrow. Give me a ring about six and I'll tell you what I've found out."

"All right," she said. "Thanks." She found it hard to look at him, felt somehow ashamed that she could hurt him with a word, dismissing him. But she had to look at him, had to see his dark nervous eyes, his painful smile, see him wave and hear him say: "I hope it keeps fine for you." He turned away, hurrying on down the road with his half-running stride.

And so she went into the park. The path she took was on the edge of the zoo and the animals were separated from her by a kind of moat. On her left Barbary sheep looked down on her from a high concrete cliff ledge. To her right was a huge park meadow. Dogs and their owners used this grassy place, the dogs running joyously wild, leash-trained city dogs enjoying their moment of release. She walked on slowly, aware that the rest of the afternoon was hers. She had been set free in this park, granted this time alone. As she continued on down the path, she passed the elephant house. Standing on a concrete ramp, swaying, was an old lizard-colored elephant, its trunk reaching into the air as though to pluck out invisible buns. The elephant turned in her direction, looking at her across the moat. Its ears came up like kites, then fell slap against its gray lizard cheeks. Ponderously lifting and shifting its prehistoric legs, it moved with a prisoner's aimless deliberation back into the elephant house. She walked on, passing a part of the zoo which seemed to be for children and was a farm with ordinary farm animals penned in, so that city children could come and touch them and play with them. She watched an attendant let a little girl feel the fleece of a lamb. She remembered seeing sheep shorn and dipped on a farm in Donegal. It was a cold and brutal sight, the shearers throwing the thick fleeces to one side; the naked, wet, shivering animals herded down wooden chutes; the acrid smell of disinfectant in the sheep dip.

She came out into another part of the park, a wide avenue with trees on either side and on the edge of the meadow the park railings and behind them the white Regency mansions Bernard had pointed out to her the other day when they drove up to Kenwood House. As she walked, the sky overhead seemed to darken. She hoped it would not rain. She did not want to go back to the hotel but to stay here in the park as long as possible. There was a bench up ahead and she sat on it. Pigeons pecked close, then jibbed away, finding no food near her feet. She looked up at the line of trees bordering her walk, then looked down the path and saw someone moving there, some man in a raincoat. She saw him dodge behind a tree as if to hide himself from her. The way he moved was familiar, the angular tilt to his shoulders. Bernard. Imagine Bernard McAuley of all people hiding behind a tree here in a London park. And not in a game, either, not in a joke at all. But serious.

As she watched him hiding, not knowing that she had seen him, she decided to teach him a lesson, to leave him here, not knowing where she had gone. She was wearing summer sandals. Surreptitiously, she kicked them off, then slipped them in her raincoat pocket. She looked at the great meadow of grass to her left, and there on the other side of the park she saw bushes and distant trees. She stood up and stepped on the grass, feeling its pleasant dampness on her bare soles. She began to run, easily at first, but as she went into the great expanse of meadow, she ran like the unleashed dogs she had just seen, free and wild, her head up, her hair streaming out behind her, running barefoot across the meadow. She did not look back. She knew he would follow. And then he fell out of her mind as all thought did, as she rushed, panting, headlong, seeing the surprised looks of lovers and loiterers lying in the grass as she fled past them, seeing a collie, which began to run after her, seeing three boys kicking a football stop to stare and start to laugh at the sight of her. Ran across the great meadow, running toward bushes and far-off park railings, free as she had not been since she came here. She felt the beginnings of a stitch in her side, but then got her second wind and reached the bushes and an asphalt-covered path which led along the edge of the park. She ran down this path, running toward high shrubbery, behind which she would be lost to the sight of anyone following her across the meadow. She thought for a moment of running right out of the park, but then came to a turn in the path, saw a bank of flowers and, beyond it, bushes where she could hide. She ran to cover, throwing herself down on a grassy bank behind the bushes, panting, lying full-length, looking out through the bushes as though she were a child playing hide and seek.

At first, from her blinkered perspective through the bushes, the great expanse of meadow seemed empty. Then, in the distance, she saw children flying kites. Gradually, more people came into her line of vision. Among them was a runner. The runner was Bernard and she saw that he was running in the general direction she had taken. She saw him stop and look about, a small lonely figure in the great expanse of meadow and sky, the lost dog she had imagined. He came on, running again, going in the direction of the path she had taken. She realized that if he kept on his present course he would pass by her hiding place. He ran erratically but at a speed which, had he been sure of his direction, would have kept him on her heels. As he came closer, he slowed and looked around, searching for her. She saw his face. She had never seen him like this. His face was the face of a man distraught as from some awful news. His dark eyes darted this way and that as though someone might attack him. He panted from the exertion of running, his bony chest heaved, his mouth was slack and open as though someone had punched him in the stomach and he was about to fall down from the blow. At about twenty yards from her he stopped and stood, swaying slightly, like a man about to faint. He lowered his head as though in despair. And as she lay there on her stomach, the sandals in her pocket pressing uncomfortably against her hip, staring at him through the bushes as though she were a sniper and he her innocent victim, she felt a strange sad empathy for Bernard McAuley. For how terrible it must be to fall in love with someone who was completely out of the question, someone who turned from you in disgust, someone who would never ever acknowledge one bit of the love you felt for them.

And there, in the park, watching him, she admitted to herself that he did love her and could not help himself. No one had ever loved her like this, perhaps no one ever would again. If she had been like Mona, someone who all her life had boys running after her, then Bernard would just be another suitor, common as a day of the week. But for her, who had never had a real boy friend, it was easy to put herself in Bernard's place. What if, someday, she too fell hopelessly in love with someone who had no time for her. If that ever happened, would she remember the way she had behaved today?

Bernard sat down. He did not pick a place to sit, he sat. For a moment he sat normally and then, as though faint, fell back, his arms outstretched, lying flat on the grass, looking up at the orb of sky. He seemed unaware that the grass was wet, and this was so unlike him, who was so careful of his clothes, that she stood up, worried that there was something wrong with him, looking at him over the tops of the bushes. She reached in her pocket, put on her sandals, and without consciously thinking of a plan of action came out from the bushes near the place where she had taken cover. It was then that she decided to walk past him, close enough for him to see her, but pretending she had not seen him. She did this, passing close to him. He lay, staring at the sky. He was not pretending. He had not seen her. She walked back to him and said, "What are you doing here?"

He sat up, smiling a victim's smile as though telling her he knew she was lying. "I've been running," he said. "But I'm afraid I don't have your speed."

"I thought you were going to let me go for a walk on my own?"

"I can't help myself. You're my magnet. I was just lying here thinking: What if she goes and marries someone. Will that make a difference? And I decided, No."

She laughed, embarrassed. "Of course it would. You'd soon get over it, in that case."

"No. I'd still love you. I will always love you."

To her left, through the park railings, she saw a stream of taxis rushing by on the road. The words he had spoken sounded in her head. *I'd still love you. I will always love you.* She saw herself years from now, in Ireland, in Belfast or Dublin, married and out walking a pram with a child in it and there, in the street, would come walking toward her, Bernard McAuley, older than now, and his face would light up at the sight of her and they would have some awkward chat and he would pretend to admire her baby. *I will always love you.* To have some man, any man, love you all his life without you ever kissing him or giving him a kind word. She looked down at him, at his bald spot. God help him.

"But supposing I went away someplace," she said. "Supposing you never saw me for years and years?"

"That wouldn't change anything. Don't you see, I can't go back now to the life I had before I met you.

Loving you is all I have. If I stopped loving you, I'd kill myself."

"Oh, for goodness' sake. Don't say things like that, even as a joke."

"I'm not joking."

"That's ridiculous," she said. "When I think of people like my mother trying to hang on to what bit of life they have left, I haven't time to be listening to any old rubbish about killing yourself."

"I see." He looked up at her. "Yes, I'm ridiculous, I know I am. All right, go on, you don't have to stay here. Go back to the hotel." He got up from the wet grass and went over and sat on an empty park bench at the side of the path. She looked at him sitting there, sorry for himself. Good riddance. She was about to make off as fast as she could when she noticed his face. There was something in his face, something that frightened her. He looked like someone who might do something terrible. She went up to him. "Come on," she said. "Don't be silly. You know what I meant. I never said you were ridiculous. I said talking about killing yourself is ridiculous. It's not the same thing."

But he did not look at her. She sat down beside him. Some leaves dragged past, blown by a sudden gust. A leaf stuck to his trouser leg. He looked at the leaf, then reached down and picked it off. He held the leaf in his hand, looking at it. It was as though she were no longer with him. She moved closer to him, almost touching him. For a time, neither of them spoke. Then he raised his head and looked straight ahead. "Of course it's ridiculous," he said. "A man in the state I'm in isn't to be pitied. He's a walking joke. He's laughable, isn't he, Eileen?"

"No, he's not."

"I should let you go," he said. "The only thing I should think about now is how to make you happy." He turned and looked at her for the first time since he had sat on the bench. "To make you happy," he repeated. "That's what I want."

"I know that," she said, wanting to cheer him up. But the moment she spoke he stood up, buttoning his coat. "Maybe I'm lying to myself," he said. "Maybe it's not what I want. After all, you're trying to run away from me. Everything has changed. And when things change they can't be changed back. If that's the case, then God help you." He turned to her and she saw tears in his eyes. "I mean, God help you, because I can't help anyone now. I can only hurt them. Come on. Let's go out and find a taxi. I'll give you a lift back to the hotel."

She went with him, the two of them walking side by side toward the park gate. She thought of the look she had seen on his face, the look that frightened her. I'll go back with him now, she said to herself. But I'd better find Mona and tell her. He's her husband, he's her responsibility, not mine. And she wants to keep him: she wants things to stay as they are. It's her worry. Tomorrow, I'll ask her for my ticket and go home. Away from this.

She watched him walk toward the gleaming white Regency houses in the crescent, watched as he walked dangerously into the traffic, ignoring the car horns and squealing brakes and the curses of a taxi driver. He stood there in the middle of the road, holding up his hand until a cab stopped and pulled into the curb.

"Ready?" he called to her as he held the cab door open. He told the driver the name of the hotel, then climbed in beside her, avoiding her, sitting in the corner, staring out the window. They did not speak during the journey back. When they arrived at the hotel and he had paid off the taxi, they went together into the lobby. She turned to him. "Where's Mona?" she said.

"Is she in, do you think? Should we have a cup of tea, maybe?"

But he ignored this. He fumbled with the inside pocket of his jacket and took out an envelope. "Here are those theater tickets for tonight," he said. "You might like to go on your own. Do you have money? You could have an early supper here in the hotel."

She took the tickets. She did not know what else to do. "I'd like to see Mona," she said. "Do you think she's in?"

"I'll find out." He went to the house telephones, then came back. "She'll be down in a minute," he said. "I'll leave the two of you to your tea."

"You don't want tea?" she asked, foolishly, for, of course, she wanted to speak to Mona on her own.

"You don't want me," he said and went away to the lifts. She watched him waiting there, his shoulders hunched. *I will always love you.* The lift came and he got in. She walked across the lobby, and as she did she saw the American girl, the baby's mother, having coffee in the lounge with a tall, very good-looking boy who was dressed, as she was, in jeans and a checked shirt. At once, the American girl waved, inviting Eileen over.

"Hi, how are you? How's it going? This is Bill, my husband."

"Hi, there," Bill said, smiling pleasantly. He had beautiful eyes, Eileen thought. They seemed both green and blue.

"This is the girl I was telling you about," Arlene said to her husband. "The Irish girl I thought was the Wales girl."

"Did you get a sitter?" Eileen asked.

"Well, sort of. I mean that Wales agency is something else. They sent a woman, finally, and she's with the baby now, but she has to leave at five and after that we're on our own. They just can't help us."

"You wouldn't like to do some baby-sitting, would you?" Bill asked, smiling to show he was joking.

"Anyway," Arlene said, "we have our friend who's living here, he's still trying to find someone for us. We're just keeping our fingers crossed. We have tickets to this Shakespeare play that starts at seven."

"Well, good luck," Eileen said.

"Thanks."

Eileen went back into the lobby. The American girl was not even good-looking, yet she had that really nice and nice-looking husband and a lovely baby. And as she was thinking about the husband and his astonishing eyes, she saw Mona at the porter's desk, wearing an overcoat as though she were about to go out. Mona saw her and waved to her. They met. "Bernard said you wanted to have tea?"

"Yes, I told him that because I wanted to have a word with you."

"Well, let's have tea, then," Mona said and led her back into the lounge. A waiter came up at once. "Do you want anything with your tea?" Mona asked, and when Eileen said no, Mona said to the waiter, "Bring us one cup of tea and a double vodka-and-tonic." She took a package of cigarettes from her purse and lit one, a surprise, for she had given up smoking six months ago. "What happened at the airport?" she asked.

"Nothing. I didn't get out."

"Did you have lunch?"

"Oh, we met some friends of Bernard's at the airport and they gave us a lift back and we had lunch at their house."

"What friends?"

"Irwin was their name."

"Oh, them. And what happened after that? I mean, what did you do this afternoon?"

"We walked in the park. That's what I want to talk to you about. I'm worried about Bernard."

"*You're* worried?" Mona laughed an angry laugh. "That's a good one."

"Look, this isn't my fault, you know."

"Not your fault. Well, and whose fault is it, then? You that didn't have the decency to wait till Sunday to go home. It's your behavior that's driving him around the bend, isn't it? Do you know what he said to me just now when he came up to the room? He said, 'Go downstairs and have tea with Eileen. And, after that, get out.' I said to him: 'What are you talking about?' and he said: 'Go out and stay out, and when you come back tonight, go straight into the bedroom. I'll sleep on the sofa in the living room and I don't want to be disturbed. In fact, I don't want you to speak to me between now and the time we go home unless I speak to you first.' Well, you know, normally I'd tell him to go and take a running jump at himself, but he's like somebody who would knock you down if you crossed him. In fact, he hit me this morning. For the first time in our marriage. He hit me. That's what you've brought on us, you that I gave a job to, you that I promoted and treated like nobody else that works for us, that I made a pet of as if you were my own kid sister. You that turned out to be as cold as charity."

"There's no good putting all this on me," Eileen said. "Whatever is wrong must have been wrong before I came along. It's not just me."

"Well, for your information it is just you."

"That's not true," Eileen said, losing her temper. "Is it because of me you were making eyes at total strangers the other night in this lounge?"

"Who was making eyes? What are you talking about? I'm not like you, I don't have to make eyes."

The waiter came with the tea and the vodka-and-tonic.

[127]

Mona had to sign the chit. "Was it Bernard who told you I was making eyes?"

"I saw you myself."

"Oh, did you now? And what did you see?"

"Never mind."

"Well, I do mind. I have no notion of what you're talking about. I'm telling you, I'll not let you get away with this. Oh, I can just see it, you'll be trying to blacken the two of us at home, telling lies just because poor Bernard who never played around with anybody in his whole life was stupid enough to fall for the likes of you. Well, if you say anything about me at home, if you say it to a single soul, mind, I'll make damn sure that everybody knows how much you took from us and how much you led Bernard on."

"I never led him on," Eileen said, outraged. "God, what a liar you are, Mona." And rose, wanting to get away from this, afraid of the spite and rage on Mona's face, but as she got up Mona got up too, almost spilling over the tea and the vodka-and-tonic, catching hold of Eileen's sleeve, detaining her. "Oh, wait, wait, I'm sorry. Listen, I *am* sorry, I don't know what happened to me, it's just that this carry-on of Bernard's is driving me mad and I tried to take it out on you, which isn't fair; of course you never led him on, you never knew what was going on, how could you? I didn't mean it, honestly. It's just that I don't want the whole blinking world knowing about this."

"And do you think I want people to know about it?" Eileen said, but allowed Mona to make her sit down again.

"Of course not, of course you don't," Mona said. She picked up her drink and drank some of it. "Oh, God, what am I going to do, I'm so worried about him. I mean, he'll not listen to me. He hates me now. Once he heard you were leaving, he changed into some sort of mad person. That's why I have to go out. He's ordered me out."

Eileen said nothing. She thought of Mona on the house telephone the other evening and Bernard coming down, making way for the stranger she took upstairs with her. Surely he hated her long before this.

"And what are you going to do this evening?" Mona asked.

"He gave me theater tickets and told me to go on my own."

"Why don't you ask him to take you? It wouldn't kill you. And he'd love that."

"I don't want to," Eileen said. "I don't want to be with him." Tears came into her eyes.

"All right, all right, I'm not forcing you. Do what you want. Go out and enjoy yourself. That's what I'm going to try to do." Mona stood up. "I suppose you think I'm off to pick somebody up. Wasn't that what you said? Well, for your information, I'm going to see Tess, my friend that I went to Queen's with. Thank God, I have a friend I can go to, to get away from this madness for an hour or two. I'd advise you to do the same. Go to the theater. Are you going to go through that rigmarole of trying to get home again tomorrow?"

"Mona," Eileen said. "I suppose you wouldn't think of lending me the money for an air ticket? If you would, I could go out to the airport tonight and stay out there until I got a flight. That's really what I want to do."

"God," said Mona. "Are you as thick as I think you are? Bernard has your ticket, right?"

"Yes, that's the trouble."

"Well, ring him up and ask him for it."

"I don't think he'd give it to me. He'd insist on driving me out there."

"So you think that, do you? And do you think he'd be delighted with me if I gave you the money for another ticket behind his back? Are you daft?" Mona said, and, dismissing her, turned and walked out of the lounge, moving quickly, legs, hips, swing of shoulder choreographing her angry rejection of Eileen's stupidity. Eileen stared at the untasted cup of tea. She put sugar and milk in it and sipped it, not because she wanted it, but because it had been bought and paid for. The tea was cold. She looked around the lounge, which had begun to fill up with the group of elderly American tourists she had seen earlier in the day. Some of the poor old things were standing about not finding seats, so she got up, smiled at three old ladies, and pointed to her vacant table. "Oh, thank you, thanks a lot," the old ladies said in their flat American voices, and Eileen, moving away, walked toward the lobby exit, where she saw the American husband, Bill, still sitting at his table. His wife was no longer with him, but on her chair was the baby carrier with the baby in it. Eileen stopped and smiled down at the baby. "Any luck?"

He shook his head. "Arlene's gone off to try another agency on the phone. But we've only got an hour to find someone. So it doesn't look good."

"I'll sit for you," she said. The words came out of her unthinkingly, but the moment she said it she knew it was what she wanted to do. She could stay in their room with the baby and watch telly all evening and Bernard would never find her. Whereas, if she went to the theater, he would probably follow her there and be waiting for her when she came out.

"You're not serious?" the American boy asked.

"I am. I'm not doing anything special this evening." She sat down, lifting the carrier and placing it on her knees. The baby looked up, its glistening eyes seeming to see her. She put out her finger and the baby caught and held it in its tiny fist.

"That's fantastic," the American boy said. "Are you sure?"

"Yes, of course."

"Well, I'll go get Arlene. What about your supper?"

"I'll order something up in the room."

"Okay, good. You put it on our bill, okay?" He stood up, excited, and, after a moment's hesitation, turned and raced off across the lobby to find his wife. Eileen let the baby hold her finger. To do something for other people instead of always taking. The baby gurgled and a little spittle oozed from its rosy lips. She took its bib and wiped its chin. And then, hurrying, the pair of them very excited, Arlene came back with Bill.

"Listen, this is really nice of you."

"Oh, it's no trouble."

"You're sure?"

"Watch it, Arlene," Bill said, laughing. "Don't give her a chance to change her mind."

And so the three of them went up in the lift with the baby, Arlene saying that she'd "struck out" on getting anybody from any of the agencies she'd tried, and beginning to explain about the baby's formula and when it was to be fed. Their room was bigger than the new room Eileen had moved to and had an alcove off the main bedroom in which the baby's cot was set up. There was a great deal of luggage stacked up along one wall and in the bathroom Arlene had laid out all the stuff for the baby, formula and diapers. She explained it all very clearly to Eileen while Bill put on a jacket and tie. Then, while Arlene was getting into a dress in the bathroom, Bill said, "We'll pay you, of course. This is really terrific."

"No, no need."

"Oh, we must. And your supper. Listen, here's the room-service card. Just order from it and I'll tell the desk to put it on my account, okay?"

Arlene came out, looking quite different in a dress, older but prettier. "Oh, wow!" she said suddenly "What about Earl? Can you contact him?"

"No way," her husband said. He turned to Eileen. "This friend of mine, Earl, he was the one was supposed to get us a sitter in the first place. Anyway, he said he would phone before seven and he'd sit for us if we couldn't get anybody else. I told him no." And here Bill laughed. "Frankly, we didn't like the idea of leaving him as baby sitter. It's not his act. Okay, so he may phone the room to find out if we got anybody. So you can tell him we got you."

"All right," Eileen said. "Have a good time and don't worry about getting home late. It's easy for me. I just have to go upstairs to my own room."

"Oh, that's so sweet," Arlene said and kissed Eileen on the cheek and hugged her. And Bill smiled his handsome smile and put his arm around Eileen's shoulder in a brotherly half hug.

"Thanks, thanks a lot," he said.

The door shut. She was alone in a London hotel room with a baby. And it came to her that at that moment nobody except these two Americans knew where she was, not even her own mother. Then remembered that, earlier this week, she had told Mama she would ring her today. She did not want to ring her now, not after all this, but what if Mama rang the hotel? She lifted the receiver and got the hotel operator. "This is Miss Hughes and my room number is 203. But I won't be in my own room this evening I'll be in 402. I'm expecting a phone call from Ireland, so if it comes, can you put it through to 402?"

"Yes, miss. Very good, miss."

Was the operator surprised that she was spending the evening in someone else's room? She thought not. Not when they had guests like Mona. The baby began to cry. She picked it up and held it, and it stopped. She walked across the room, rocking it in her arms as she had seen mothers do. It felt so tiny and fragile. Imagine if she had a little baby like this. Its eyes were closed now and she kissed its soft cheek and laid it back in its cot, then lowered the room lights and looked at the bedside clock. Twenty to seven. She sat in the chair closest to the television set and switched the channel on. It was some sort of science program. She left it on low but found herself not listening to it. She thought of Bernard this afternoon in the park, sitting on the damp grass. *I'd still love you. I will always love you.* Was Mona right that she had led him on? Could a person be guilty of a thing even if they didn't know they were doing it? She felt shame when she thought of him hitting Mona because of her. *For the first time in our marriage. He hit me. That's what you've brought on us.* Of course, you could not believe Mona. He must have had plenty of reason to hit her before now, her and her men. But still.

Someone was knocking on the door. She got up in a hurry: she didn't want the baby to waken. When she unlocked it, there, smiling at her, was a young man, and the first thing she thought about this young man was that he was like an actor in a cowboy film. He was tall and slim with long, dark hair and a long, curling mustache. He wore faded blue jeans, pointy Western boots, a fringed leather shirt, and a leather belt inlaid with silver ornaments and turquoise stones. On his shoulder was a canvas pouch, and now as he faced her, his hands rested on his hips like a gunfighter about to draw. His small merry eyes were amused. "Am I in the wrong place? I'm looking for the Simmondses."

"No, this is their room. They're out, though."

"Then you must be the baby sitter, right?"

"Yes."

He grinned, as though delighted. "Well, then, that makes two of us. How's our baby?"

"Are you this friend of theirs? Earl?"

"Yes, indeedy. And I can tell you're Irish."

"Yes, I am."

"Well, if you're Irish, come into the parlor," he sang and went past her into the darkened room. He approached the baby's cot, put his finger to his lips, then bent down to look at the baby. She liked him, liked his merry eyes, his air of high spirits and conspiracy. He turned from the cot and came to her. "Hey, it's a real cute baby," he whispered. "And so's its sitter. How did they find you?"

"They didn't. I'm staying in the hotel and I offered. I felt sorry for them, just the two days in London and not able to go out."

"Well, that was really sweet," he said. He sat on the double bed and put down his shoulder bag. "Here I was all set to be the Good Samaritan and you beat me to it. What's your name?"

"Eileen. Eileen Hughes."

"And you live in London?"

"No, I'm just on holiday."

"You're beautiful."

"Oh, go on," she said, and felt herself flush.

"I am always sincere," he said. He opened his shoulder bag and produced a bottle of wine. "Go look in the bathroom and see if they have another glass," he said. "I only have one glass. I thought I'd be spending the evening alone. You'll join me in a glass of wine, won't you?"

"Oh, no, that's all right."

He stood up, went into the bathroom, and came back

with a small tumbler. He uncorked the wine and poured some in the tumbler and into a wineglass which he took from his bag. He handed her the tumbler and held his own glass up in toast. "Here's to us baby sitters," he said. They drank. He sat again on the bed. She sat in the armchair, but only after going into the alcove to make sure the baby was asleep. "We mustn't wake her," she warned him.

"Of course. Although I'd like to keep you company for a while. I mean, I was all set to spend my evening here. What's your sign?"

"My what?"

"Astrological sign. When were you born, what day and month?"

"The fifteenth of September."

"Virgo," he said. "So that's all right. I'm Taurus. We'll be good together." He felt in his jeans pocket and took out a small tin box. From the box he took a wizened cigarette and lit it. She had seen that sort of cigarette before, seen them in the back of the shop, the drivers and stockroom boys smoking them. He drew on the cigarette and offered it to her.

"Oh, no, thanks."

"Come on," he said. "This is really good stuff. Try it. It won't hurt you."

"I'd rather not. I've never had one."

"You never?" He seemed surprised. "You're kidding."

"No."

"Ireland must be something else," he said. "Listen, I'll make a deal with you. Just take one puff now and one later. Like a cigarette. Inhale it. Okay?"

"No, thanks," she said, but he stood over her, merry and smiling, and there was no harm in him, he wasn't threatening her. She liked him, and what harm, she had thought of trying it before, so she took a puff and coughed and it tasted like a cigarette. He showed her how to puff it properly and take it into her lungs. Then he sat by her and asked where she came from in Ireland, and soon they were chatting as if they had known each other for a long while. He told her he was an A and R man and said he had been working in London for the past six months. She asked what was an A and R man and he laughed and said he worked for a record company. He said he and Bill, Arlene's husband, had been at U.C.L.A. together, but she didn't ask what U.C.L.A. was. She felt if she had to ask everything he would think her stupid. She thought he was about twenty-six or -seven. He said he traveled a lot in his job and had to go to Paris and Germany once a month. She said that must be a terrible hardship and they both laughed and he had her take another puff or two of the cigarette. Then he asked what she did and she said she worked in a shop but that she was hoping to make a change soon and maybe try to train as a nurse. And when she said that, he lay back in the bed at once and asked her if she knew how to take a pulse. He took his own pulse and told her he was coming down with something. "With a cold?" she asked innocently, and he laughed again and said in a loud voice, "No, it's more serious. I've got an advanced case of baby sitter." And she had to shush him for fear of waking the baby, and when she went to the alcove to look at the baby, Earl came up behind her and, in an easy way no Irish boy would have, put his arms around her, both of them looking down at the sleeping baby, and turned to her, smiling with his conspirator's eyes. And she sensed then that he would like to kiss her but that he would not do anything you did not want him to do. And again, in that easy way, he walked her back to the bed and said: "Let's sit on the bed."

"You sit on it," she said. "I like the armchair. Anyway, there's no need for you to stay, you know."

"I know. I'd just like to visit with you for a while."
And he lay full-length on the bed, finishing his twisty
butt while she went and sat in the armchair.

"I bet you have a boy friend in Ireland."

"No."

"I can't believe it."

"Well, I don't have a steady boy friend," she said, to
make it sound better.

"Not ready to settle down yet, right?"

"I suppose."

He smiled, raised himself on an elbow, and poured
more wine in their glasses. "Someday I'm going back to
L.A., get me a place at the beach, and raise a family.
Someday." He sipped his wine and reached in his
fringed shirt to produce his little metal box. Dreamy-
eyed, he lit another of his cigarettes. "Yes, I like babies,"
he said. "And I never thought baby-sitting could be so
neat." He reached the new cigarette in her direction.

"No, no," she said, but he kept nodding, his eyes
twinkling conspiratorially, and the first cigarette had
not had any effect on her, so when he said: "Just one
drag, okay?" she didn't want to offend him and took a
puff, inhaling as he had said and holding the smoke inside her. She had been waiting for it to make her drunk,
but suddenly with this puff she sensed that it was not
going to be at all like drink. It was not at all like drink
because whatever was happening or had already happened, she was not drunk but at ease the way Earl was
at ease: easy as she had not been all week since she arrived in London. And so when he moved over on the
bed and patted a place for her to lie down and join
him, she wasn't cross or afraid of him, but just smiled
the way he did and shook her head, and he nodded,
accepting her decision, and held out the cigarette to her
and she took another puff. She could not believe it but
the thing about this stuff was that you did not think of

things the way you normally would. Everything was slow and nice and now, while she did not go to lie on the bed with him, she got up to hand him back the cigarette and sat on the edge of the bed, smiling down at him, smiling as he told her he would go to Ireland some weekend and look her up. He asked if she would be at home or did she travel a lot, and she found herself telling him that this was the first time she had ever been out of Ireland. "No kidding," he said. "Hey, why don't you come to Paris next time I go over? That's a good town, you know."

"I've always wanted to go to Paris."

"Well, why don't you? It's just a short hop."

"For you, maybe. But it costs too much for the likes of me."

"I'm going over next week," he said. "Wednesday." He lay staring up at the ceiling and puffing his cigarette. She sat beside him, at ease. It was not like any conversation she had ever had before. You talked only if you felt like talking. It was nice. She thought about Paris. Now that she was in London, Paris seemed not just a place she dreamed about but a real place, a place you could go to tomorrow on a plane.

"Listen," he said suddenly. "Why don't you come with me next week? I'm on expenses, I can take care of it. Know what we'll do? The first night we'll go on one of those dumb dinner cruises, we'll sit on deck eating our dinner and cruising along the Seine past Notre-Dame and all that stuff, like real tourists. I'm crazy about that river. Know what I do when I'm in Paris? I swim in those big floating dock pools on the Seine. I like that."

For a time she said nothing. She was thinking about Earl and herself in one of those boats. She knew about those boats from a big picture book on Paris that Mona had lent her. "They're called *bateaux-mouches*," she said.

"Right. *Bateaux-mouches.* I thought you didn't know Paris."

"You don't have to go to a place to know about it."

"Profound observation," Earl said and sucked hard on the tiny end of his cigarette. He stretched out a lazy arm. "Pass me that phone, will you, hon?"

She handed him the receiver. "What's the room number, again?" he asked her, and then he asked for room service and ordered a bottle of wine and two glasses. He leaned across her and let the receiver slide back on its cradle. "So," he said. "Next Wednesday. And speaking of wine, we'll leave on a lunchtime flight. A little champagne lunch on the plane. How does that hit you, kid?"

She laughed: it wasn't funny but it seemed funny. "It doesn't hit me at all," she said. "I just swore off free trips. Sooner or later you pay for things."

"Mnnnn," Earl sang and lay back with his eyes shut. "There's no free lunch. Gotcha. Still . . ." His voice trailed away, and for a minute she thought he had fallen asleep. "It beats working, though," he said. "When I was a kid I lived right next to the First Baptist Church of Studio City. Minister there had a big billboard on the corner lot beside his church. WAGES OF SIN IS DEATH. Big, big letters. I used to pass it on the way to school. Then one morning I looked up and saw that somebody had Day-gloed out DEATH and put in FUN instead. I thought that was an improvement. *That* was gospel truth." He turned and looked at her with merry eyes. "That's my position on the free-lunch issue."

She smiled. There was a knock on the door and it was a waiter with wine and two glasses on a white-napkined tray. Earl paid with a bundle of pound notes which he took from the hip pocket of his jeans.

"No more wine for me," she said, when the waiter had gone. "I'll be drunk."

"Well, pour me a measure, will you," Earl said. "Be

my baby sitter. Listen, maybe I can hire you to baby-sit me for a couple of days in Paris. That would solve the free trip issue, right?"

"But I'm not really a baby sitter." She got up and poured wine in a glass and brought it to him. "Besides, I'm going home tomorrow, I hope."

He took the glass but did not drink. Instead, he set it on the bed table and, reaching up, took hold of her wrist in his gentle way. "Why are you going home?" he said. "End of your vacation? Or don't you like London?"

"Oh, it's too long to explain."

He drew her down gently so that she was again sitting on the edge of the bed. "You mean I might never see you again. That we might just meet this one night of our lives?"

"I suppose so."

"I find that sad," he said. "Listen. Would you give me a kiss? Just a therapeutic little kiss? Or maybe that's asking too much?"

She looked at him, at his fringed shirt, his long, curling mustache, his dark hair falling about his shoulders. If only someone like this would fall madly in love with her. She leaned toward him and, awkwardly, put her lips in a pout, ready to be kissed. He sat up, put his arm around her, and kissed her, first on the lips, then on her cheek, then on her neck. His kisses gave her a tingling sensation, both pleasant and shivery: he was gentle and warm and she felt excited and not afraid, for when he had kissed her neck he did not try to put his hand up between her legs as an Irish boy would have done, but just sat with his arms around her, smiling at her. "Thank you," he said. "That was nice. I really liked that. Thank you."

And then, she did not know why, she leaned toward him and kissed him on the lips, her mouth open, holding him. After a moment he released her, picked up the new wine, drank from the glass, and savored it. "Not bad," he said. "Sure you won't try a glass?"

"I'd be drunk. Maybe I am drunk, who knows?"

"You're not drunk. You may be getting a little stoned, but that's okay. I wonder when was the first time I got stoned. I guess I was about nine or ten."

"You're joking."

"No, I was a late developer." He cocked his head. "Is that the door?"

It was. Someone knocked a second time.

"Somebody for you?" Earl asked.

"No."

"I'll go." He went in his gunfighter, heel-rocking way to the door. He opened and she heard him say "Who?"

And then, loud and anxious, Bernard's voice: "Miss Hughes. Miss Eileen Hughes?"

"Well, we do have an Eileen here," Earl said, turning to her. "Somebody for you."

The drug protected her. She found herself wondering how he had found her. And now he came in through the doorway, his face very pale, his nervous dark eyes darting around the room. "What is this, what are you doing here?" he asked, the words tumbling out of him.

"I'm baby-sitting."

"What baby?" He stared at Earl, who had gone back to the bed table and was pouring himself more wine.

"The baby's in there, in the alcove. Keep your voice down. There were some people I met here, they had no sitter. How did you find me, anyway?"

"I was trying to ring you. The operator said you were in this room. Christ!" He sniffed the air. "Is that marijuana?"

"Right," Earl said, coming over, wineglass in hand. "Hi. I'm Earl Webster."

"This is Bernard McAuley," Eileen told Earl. "He's my boss."

[141]

"Nice to meet you," Earl said. "Want to join us in a toke?"

"A what?" Bernard said. He did not seem to understand. He turned to Eileen. "Were you smoking marijuana?" he said.

She smiled at him. It was funny how far away he seemed from her this minute, as though he was somebody she had known a long time ago. "Yes," she said. "It was my first time. It's really nice."

"Oh, my God," Bernard said. He seemed dazed rather than angry. It was as though what he saw here was so completely unprecedented that his mind refused to deal with it. "But if you're baby-sitting," he said, "how could you be smoking marijuana?" He turned to Earl. "And who are you, what are you doing here?"

"I'm the back-up baby sitter," Earl said. "Maybe you'd care for some wine?"

"Eileen, can I talk to you for a minute," Bernard said. "I mean outside."

"I can't leave the baby."

"Look, why don't I step outside for a minute?" Earl said. "And give you a little privacy, okay, Eileen?"

"We won't be a moment," Eileen said.

"No hurry." Earl moved through the doorway with his gunfighter wobble. Bernard shut the door after him. His eyes were bright, and when he spoke his voice was filled with suppressed rage.

"Listen," he said, "I want you to come with me this minute. Is that his child?"

"No. He's a friend of the people I'm baby-sitting for."

"Well, let him baby-sit, then," Bernard said, almost stuttering in his anger. "You come with me."

"No. I promised these people. I'll be all right."

"What do you mean you'll be all right? You're smoking marijuana. God, how could you do a thing like this? I thought you had some decency in you, and the moment I turn my back I find you in a stranger's bedroom smoking marijuana with some bloody Yank degenerate. Do you think I want it on my conscience that because of me you've become a drug addict?"

She laughed. "It's nothing to do with you. And I haven't become a drug addict, that's silly."

"It *is* to do with me," Bernard said and held up his hands as if to push her away. She saw that his hands were trembling. "Don't lie to me. I brought you here, I'm responsible to your mother. I love you, Eileen. Please don't do this."

"Do what? Go on back to your room, Bernard. All right, I won't smoke any more of that stuff. It was wrong to do it, especially when I'm baby-sitting. But it has nothing to do with you."

"It *has* to do with me. It's because of what I said to you yesterday that all this has happened."

"Stop that," she said. As she said it she could not believe that she was talking this way to Bernard McAuley. "That's rubbish. Now, go on back to your room. You'll wake the baby with this shouting."

"To hell with the baby. I'll go and get one of the hotel maids to sit with it. It's only a matter of paying enough money. Now, you're not staying here. You're coming with me."

"I am not. Look, I don't want to have anything more to do with you, Bernard. Maybe Mona's right, maybe I did lead you on without knowing it. Well, I'm sorry if I did. But you're not going to order me around anymore, do you hear?"

"Who said you led me on? Mona said that, did she? How dare she. I never said that, I never believed it, it's not your fault at all." He caught hold of her hand. "You've nothing to be sorry about."

"Shh! Will you keep your voice down?"

"Don't you heed Mona. If I told you about Mona,

[143]

well, never mind. Listen to me. Have you had your supper? Come, and I'll get you something to eat."

"Let go of my hand. I don't want to come with you."

"What *do* you want, then?"

"I want to go home. If I'd had my ticket tonight, I'd have stayed all night at the airport, waiting."

"If I give you your ticket now, will you come with me?"

"I told you I have to mind this baby. Now go on."

"And leave you with that pothead? Not likely."

"What business is it of yours? Anyway, there's no harm in him."

"No harm in him? No harm in him, and an hour after he's met you he has you polluted with marijuana so that you can't think straight."

"It's you that can't think straight," she said, and as she said it she saw again that desperate look in his eyes.

"Well," he said. "I never thought I'd see the day when I'd have to be hard with you. You of all people, you who mean more than anything to me. But you're coming with me now, even if I have to drag you. Even if I have to hit that pothead. Listen, if you don't come with me now I'll tear up your plane ticket and you can find your own way home. Do you hear me, Eileen?"

"I hear you," she said. "God help you." She turned and ran to the door and went out. Earl was sitting on the corridor floor. He looked up at her with his merry smile. "Hi."

"Please. We've finished. Come back in."

He rose gracefully, and came back into the room where Bernard stood, staring first at Earl and then at her.

"All right, Bernard," she said. "I'd like you to go."

"You want me to tear up your plane ticket, then?"

"Do what you want. Just go."

For a moment it was as though everything had

stopped. In that frozen moment Bernard's mind seemed the only living thing in the room, that mind which raced, desperate as a tunnel rat, trapped with no exit. And then, suddenly, the baby cried in its cot, a full loud cry, filling the silence, making her turn at once and go to it. She picked the baby up, rocking it in her arms, and felt that it was wet. She went straight to the bathroom. It was as though the imperative of the baby's need had erased that other scene completely, so that as she inexpertly stripped off the diapers, washed the baby, and prepared its change, she was surprised to see Earl come in the doorway asking, "Need help?"

"No, it's all right. Though I've never done it before." She turned and looked through to the living room. "Is he still there?" she whispered.

"No, he just took off. He's your boss, right?"

"He was."

"What was all that about tearing up your airline ticket?"

"Oh, it's a long story." She finished diapering the baby. It had stopped crying, and now she picked it up and went back to its cot. "There now, there now," she crooned to the baby. The baby looked at her. She remembered being told that young babies see people only as a blur. She leaned down and kissed the baby's cheek, then tucked the covers around it. "More wine?" Earl asked.

"No, I've had too much."

"Will he tear up your ticket?"

"Oh, I don't think so. He's just bluffing." She came back and sat in the armchair by the television set. "If he did," she asked, "how long would it take to get some money sent to me from Ireland?"

"They could wire it. Don't you have a credit card of some kind?"

She shook her head. Supposing they ditched her, left

her here stranded, didn't even pay her hotel bill, how much money did Mama have at home, probably not more than a couple of hundred pounds in her Post Office savings; she never tells what money she has, but she doesn't have much. I mustn't get in a state about money. Aunt Maeve could help in a pinch. But even as she thought of Aunt Maeve, she knew that she *was* worried. She and Mama had always been short, always scrimping, and now, without the McAuleys—

"You can always crash at my place," Earl said. "I have three bedrooms."

That made her smile. Imagine, a complete stranger offering to put her up. She looked over at him, smiling, and he beckoned to her. "Come and sit here," he said, and she got up and went across the room to him, there was something about him; she remembered his kisses, how excited she had felt. There was no badness in him. He really was offering to put her up. She sat on the bed, looking down at him. He raised himself, leaning on one elbow, drinking from his glass of wine. Then, deliberately, he put the wineglass on the bed table and patted the pillow beside him. "Lie down here," he said. "Let's talk a little. Come on."

It must be the drug, she thought, but I'm not one bit afraid of him. I feel lazy, that's what I feel. It might be nice to lie down beside this boy. She slipped off her shoes and, smiling at him, lay down. Then both of them looked up at the ceiling. She thought: I am in bed with a boy for the first time in my life. His head is next to mine on the pillow.

"Yes," he said. "I have a big place here in London. It's the company flat. The rep before me was married with two little kids. That's why it's got three bedrooms. But you don't want to hear about that, do you?" He turned to her and there, startlingly close, his smiling face, curling mustache, his merry eyes. "Anyway, if you want to use it, you're entirely welcome," he said, and put his arm around her neck, as though it never occurred to him that she might protest, and then kissed her, and as her lips opened to his, she felt excited but not nervous; it was like kissing in a film, no awkward fumbling, just kissing, and his lips moved down to kiss her neck and his fingers undid the fastener at the collar of her dress so that his lips could kiss her farther down. She stiffened and said, "Oh, no," but she knew she would let him, it must be the marijuana or the wine, but she wanted him to do it. She heard him whisper in her ear, "Take your dress off." And as he whispered this he raised her to a sitting position on the bed, and now he was helping her to take off her dress, it wasn't awkward at all, and when she pulled it over her head, she felt his fingers undoing the clasp of her bra at the back, and when she pulled free of her dress, she instinctively caught at her breasts, and he turned her toward him as though to shield her from any other gaze, holding her tight, his bare chest against her breasts, and drew her down, kissing her. She was excited, she should tell him to stop, she didn't know what he was going to do now, it was her first time to go so far with a boy, in bed with him with nothing on but her panties, and as she felt him drawing his jeans down from his hips, she closed her eyes, the excitement was too much, then felt him kiss her nipple, his tongue running over it so that her nipples stood up hard, and when his hand began to draw off her panties, she said No again, but felt him touch her down there. And then he said, "Wait," and sat up and put a rubber sheath on his big penis, very fast, while she stared at it. "No worries now," he said and smiled as he lay down and drew her over on top of him, and now he was kissing her nipple again, and she felt his tongue and his greedy lips, and at the same time, he was touching her down there, his fingers working, and she could feel his stiff penis against her stomach. She could hardly bear it, she wanted him to do it, but he kept kissing her and touching her until she almost cried out with pleasure and wanting and then, when she thought he would never stop, he moved and came on top of her and she felt him come in, it was happening to her, there was no pain, just excitement, she felt hot and drunk and greedy for him, and then a sexy fainting feeling, and she shuddered and shuddered and lay still without any thoughts until, guiltily, she remembered the baby. But the baby was quiet, it was asleep. Earl leaned over her and began to kiss her again, kissing her lips, then moving down to her neck and breast, then stopping to look up at her and smile in an easy, familiar way, as though they had often done this together. And she thought with sudden delight: I'm no longer the wee innocent, this was the real thing, not some gawky boy grabbing at you. This was making love.

The phone.

Earl sat up. "I'll get it." He reached over her to pick up the receiver, but in sudden panic, she caught his arm.

"It might be my mother, she might call here." She took up the receiver and hesitated before putting it to her ear. If it's Mama how can I speak to her?

But it was Bernard.

"Eileen?"

She felt a rush of anger, but knew it was no use hanging up. He would just ring back. "Yes," she said.

"Eileen, first of all I want to tell you how sorry I am for what I said about your ticket. You're not to heed me. You're not to worry about it. I never want you to worry again on my account."

"All right," she said. "Good night."

"No, wait. There's something else I want to say. Please?"

"Bernard, I don't want to talk to you."

"Well, it's just, I'm just ringing to say goodbye. You won't be seeing me again. That's what you want, isn't it? Well, you won't have to hide from me, or run away from me. I think it's the only thing I can do for you now."

"When are you leaving?"

"Tonight. Eileen, are you there?"

"Yes, and I'm going to hang up now."

"Wait," he said. "I love you. No one will ever love you the way I do. I failed you and I'm paying for that. I'm doing this for you because I really love you. That's all I wanted to say. Goodbye."

"Good night," she said. She reached across Earl and put the receiver back on its cradle.

"Everything okay?" Earl asked.

"Yes. Wouldn't you know he'd phone at a time like this?" she said and, angry, lay down beside Earl. But Earl understood. He turned toward her, taking her in his arms, holding her, comforting her. Wasn't it just like Bernard, always thinking of himself, announcing he was going away, making himself important. *You won't be seeing me again.* Who cares? *You won't have to hide from me, or run away from me.* But how will I not have to hide from him if the two of us are living in Lismore, sooner or later I'll bump into him. He's leaving tonight.

"You're beautiful," Earl said, beginning to kiss her again. "And sexy."

"Am I?" she said, pleased. But Bernard's face came up, the face she had seen in the park, his hair askew, that look that frightened her. "Oh, my God"

"What's the matter?" Earl raised her in the bed. "Are you okay?"

"Yes, but listen. Will you stay here and mind the baby for a minute until I come back? I won't be long."

"What's wrong?"

"Nothing, I hope." She found her dress and pulled it on over her head, found her shoes. "I'll hurry back," she said, and looked at him, Earl, who looked at her. She wanted to kiss him again.

"Do that," he said and she ran out of the room, ran to the lifts but didn't wait, and, instead, took the stairs, hurrying up three flights and coming out on the McAuleys' floor. She ran along the corridor to the end suite and knocked on the sitting-room door. Answer, please answer. Her heart lifted at the sound of footsteps. Bernard opened the door, looked surprised, then smiled, an intimate, loving smile that made her want to hit him and run downstairs again. "Come in," he said. "So you came."

"Are you all right?"

He turned, as though to lead her into the sitting room, and as he did, she saw him stagger slightly. She went in the doorway after him. All the lights were on: the room was very bright. She saw a writing table and on it was a whiskey bottle, a third empty. He was drunk, that was it. But she knew that Bernard never got drunk. "What did you mean, you were leaving tonight?" she said.

He sat down heavily in an armchair. "Yes. I'm leaving tonight."

"Bernard, do you remember what you said in the park today? You wouldn't do anything stupid, would you?"

"Stupid? No, I think it's the only intelligent solution."

"Oh, will you stop that." She felt like striking him. "Are you getting drunk, or what?" she said, and as she spoke she saw the other bottle on the floor, beneath the desk, a pill bottle, half empty. She went to it and picked it up: it was a prescription bottle: the pills were red. She looked at him again. His eyes were heavy-lidded. He smiled at her.

"Telepathy," he said. "It was telepathy sent you here. Sit for a minute, Eileen. Sit with me. Please."

"Have you taken some of these? Answer me. Have you?"

"Fifteen."

"Oh, my God. When?"

"About . . ." He pulled back his sweater sleeve and looked at his wristwatch. He seemed to have trouble seeing the dial. "About . . . ten minutes ago."

"We'll have to get a doctor." She felt her heart begin to hammer. "What's the name of that friend of yours, Irwin? Do you have his number?"

"Those are his pills. I got the prescription today. But I don't want a doctor."

"I'm not going to let you lie down and die."

"Why not? It solves everything, doesn't it?" He yawned hugely and slumped in the armchair. She ran to him and shook him. "Bernard, listen to me." What could she say to him; she felt panic, and as she shook him, trying to keep him awake, she found herself saying what the nuns had once taught her. "Listen, Bernard, do you realize that if you do this you'll go straight to hell. It's the one sin there's no forgiveness for."

He smiled sleepily. "Funny that you'd be the one to tell me that. What made you think of that?"

She thought of Earl. She went to the phone and rang the Simmondses' room.

"Don't call a doctor," Bernard said. He began to get up as if to stop her. "Don't—call—a doctor."

"I'm not." She heard Earl's voice say, "Hello."

"Earl, it's me."

"Hi, how's it going?"

"Earl, my boss has taken too many sleeping pills. What will I do?"

"Where are you? Can he walk?"

"Yes, he can walk."

"Who are you talking to?" Bernard said. "Put that phone down."

"If he can walk," Earl said, "I'll come and get him."

"But what about the baby?"

"The baby's okay. We'll bring him back to this room and work on him here. What's your room number? I'll be right up."

"Seven-five-six," she said and put the receiver down. Bernard was standing, swaying slightly, staring at her. "Who was that?" he said. "Look, don't spoil this. It's done and it's maybe the best thing I've ever done. And I'm doing it for you. That's the good thing about it."

"How are you doing it for me?" she said, just to keep him talking. "Now, don't fall asleep, Bernard." She took him by the arm. "Come on, walk up and down. Come on."

He let her lead him in a staggery walk toward the window. "I'm doing it for you," he repeated. "It's funny, but all those Christian things are true. Better to give than to receive. Giving love without expecting to be loved in return. Doing what will be best for the other person. Easy to see how people become saints. It's not hard, not hard at all."

"Stand up," she said, for he was about to sit down in a chair. She threw open the window. It was cold and rainy outside. "Put your head out," she ordered him. "Take a deep breath."

"Waste of time," Bernard said. He did not move.

"Don't be so silly," she cried at him. "Do what I tell you."

"Why?" He pulled back from her grip. "This is the best way all around. For everybody. Even for Mona."

"It's not." She held on to him. "Oh, Bernard, will you please do what I tell you. Please?"

"Look, you don't give a damn about me," he said. He pulled clear of her and went off toward the whiskey. "What do you want to keep me alive for? I'm just an embarrassment to you."

"I do care about you," she said, and as she said it, she knew she would say anything, anything that would keep him awake until Earl came.

"Ah, if only . . ." He picked up the bottle. She took it out of his hand and turned him in the direction of the open window.

"I do care, I do," she said, and as if to prove it, she kissed his cheek, although it made her flinch to touch his wet skin. He turned his beaky face toward her, blurry-eyed, as if about to descend into tears. "You kissed me. My fallible God kissed me."

By now she had him at the window. "Now, please," she said, and made him lean his head out into the cold rainy night. She heard a knock. "Come in," she called, and Earl's voice answered, "Door's locked."

"Just a minute." She released her hold on Bernard and went to open it, knowing that Bernard, without her, wouldn't stay at the window.

"What's that bloody pothead doing here? Get out, you."

"I hear you've been shooting up yourself, right?" Earl said, smiling. He went to Bernard, looked in his eyes, then picked up the bottle. "What are these?"

"Bugger off," Bernard said. "I never asked you to come in here. Go on, get out."

"Did you drink much booze?" Earl asked, ignoring this.

"I said, get him out of here," Bernard said loudly. He went toward Earl, but Eileen came between them. She put her arm around Bernard, hating him, but worried for him. "Now listen, Bernard," she said, "I want you to let us help you. If anything happened to you I'd not forgive myself. It would be terrible. I don't want anything to happen to you." She was crying, although she did not realize it. "Bernard, please. Now, do what we tell you. Please?"

He stood, letting her hold him, his eyes slate dull, his pale, bony face beaded with sweat. When he spoke his voice had thickened and slowed. "You don't want anything . . . to happen. You mean it? You don't want . . . Well, I shouldn't . . . believe you. But I want to. I'd love to." And suddenly, foolishly, he laughed and hugged her.

"Okay," Earl said. "Let's get him down to the other room. Come on, Bernard, let's go."

"Bugger off."

"Bernard!"

"Sorry," Bernard said. "Sorry, Eileen. I . . . forgot." He swayed toward Earl. "Sorry."

"That's okay," Earl said. He was much taller than Bernard, and now he seemed to tuck Bernard under his arm as he led him toward the door. "We've got to baby-sit, see? So we're going back to this other room and see what we can do for you. Come on, Eileen. Eileen's going to take your other arm, okay?"

Eileen put her arm around Bernard's waist and all three went out into the corridor. But as they went toward the stairs, Bernard balked. "I'm going with you on account of . . . Eileen. But I don't . . . I don't want a doctor. Promise now? No doctor."

"Okay," Earl said. "No doctor. Now, we're just going to walk. We won't take the elevator. Ready? You hold on to Eileen."

The hotel staircase was ahead of them, carpeted in a red pattern. The banister was of light maple wood. As they started down, Earl took most of Bernard's weight, but Bernard obstinately tried to cling to Eileen. As they went down the second flight, Bernard's breathing became loud and gasping. A hotel maid passed them, stared, then looked away, probably believing Bernard to be drunk. Eileen, her cheeks still wet with tears, saw that Earl in his free hand held the pill bottle from Bernard's room. And then, at last, they reached the Simmondses' door. Earl opened it and went in ahead of Eileen and Bernard, went straight to the cot, and looked in. "Baby's fine," he said. "Now, let me take hold of you, Bernard. Ready?"

"What?" Bernard's face was slathered in sweat. "No, let me . . . sit down. Eileen . . . I want to tell you . . . something."

"No, go with Earl. Please, Bernard. Please."

He looked at her blurrily. "I have to be dying to . . . have you talk to me like this. I never thought . . ."

"Okay," Earl said. He led Bernard into the bathroom and suddenly, like a wrestler, threw a hold around Bernard's neck. "Open your mouth," he said sharply, and as Bernard stared up at him he rammed his fingers down Bernard's throat, prising his jaws open with his other hand. He forced Bernard's head down into the sink as Bernard retched, then vomited. Bile and food particles foamed in the sink. Eileen felt like vomiting herself. Incongruously, she noticed the clean, tidy arrangement of the baby's ointments, formula, and diapers, laid out on the bathroom shelf above Bernard's vomiting head. She saw Earl put his hand in the foaming mess and retrieve two half-decomposed red pills. "How many did you take?" Earl said.

"Leave me alone."

"Eileen, hold on to him, will you."

She held Bernard's shoulders as he vomited again. She realized that in his present state he was not any stronger than she was. "How many did you take, Bernard?" Earl asked again.

"He told me fifteen," Eileen said.

"When?"

"He said about ten minutes before I came. Isn't that right, Bernard?"

But Bernard did not speak. He rested his sweating brow against the rim of the washbasin.

"Well, let's try it again," Earl said and again, ruthlessly, took hold of Bernard and thrust his fingers down his throat. This time Bernard pulled away, then vomited a few mouthfuls of brown liquid in the sink. Earl raised him and marched him out of the bathroom and up and down the bedroom. The baby woke and began to cry. "Get room service," Earl called. "The baby can wait a minute. Get room service and tell them to send up two big pots of black coffee."

She did as she was told, then went to the baby and picked it up. She walked the baby up and down the room, rocking it, at the same time as Earl was marching Bernard up and down in the opposite direction. "What sort of pills are these?" she heard Earl ask again.

"Sodium Amytal," Bernard said. "Now let me sit . . . down. I . . . I want . . . to talk to Eileen."

"Sodium Amytal." Earl took the bottle from his pocket and looked at the label. "Is this Dr. Irwin your doctor?"

"Yes, he's a friend of his, I met him today. He lives in Hampstead," Eileen said. The baby was quiet now and she laid it back in the cot.

"Said no doctor," Bernard said. "I don't want . . . I don't . . . want . . ."

Earl led Bernard to a chair and said, "Okay, you can

sit now." He signaled to Eileen to follow him into the bathroom. When she joined him he shut the bathroom door. "Unless we get a doctor, he could die on us. Now, what I want to do is keep him talking. Get him to walk if you can. I'll try to get a phone number for this Dr. Irwin. In Hampstead, you said?"

"Yes. He lives on Eaton Avenue. That was it, Eaton Avenue."

"Good. Now talk to him. Keep him awake."

She went out into the bedroom. Bernard might die. Bernard might die because of what had happened these last few days. The television set was still on, images without sound. Bernard sat in one of the chairs which faced the set, his head nodding. She went over and shook his shoulders. "Bernard," she said. "I want to ask you something. Listen to me, it's important. Can you hear me?"

He lifted his head and stared at her as though he were blind and did not see her. "Eileen?" he said. "Yes, Eileen."

"Listen, Bernard. Would you let me call a priest?"

She did not know why she said it, she wanted to say something that would keep him awake and the minute she thought that a person might be going to die, she thought of calling a priest. When her mother had her heart attack, that was the first thing she asked, Get a priest. Quick. And she had made her confession to a priest and had been anointed, there in the hospital emergency room.

"A priest?" Bernard laughed, foolishly. "Why a priest? I'm . . . I'm killing myself. I'm destroying the . . . the temple of the Holy Ghost. Right? Didn't you say yourself, that is a sin there's no forgiveness for?"

"But, Bernard, listen, listen. Stand up. Look, I'll help you." She put her arms around him and lifted him up out of the chair and stood with him in a travesty of dancing partners, her arms around him, his arms loosely draping themselves on her shoulders. "Now, listen," she said. "You know far more about these things than I do, but isn't it true that, even now, if you made your confession to a priest, if you were sorry for what you did tonight, God would forgive you. Isn't that true?"

She saw that Earl was on the phone, speaking in a low voice. Bernard had not noticed Earl. His scorn at this talk of getting a priest seemed to have revived him. "Oh, you're a funny girl," Bernard said. "Getting a priest." He smiled, then swayed and held on to her. "I'd better sit down."

"No. Listen, Bernard, would you just let me call a priest for my sake. If you won't let me call a doctor, let me at least do that." Saying it not because she meant it but just to keep him talking. She led him to the window. "Please, Bernard?"

At the window he turned to her, staring, heavy-lidded, his mind seeming to try to remember something. "Now, wait," he said, as though they were in a debate. "It's too late for a priest, even if I wanted one."

"It's not. It's *not*."

"Ah, you don't understand." He staggered, then took hold of her by the shoulders as though he were a drunken man in an argument. "Listen . . . something, something important that you don't know. It's . . . it's all over between me and God. I offered myself to God once. I wasn't wanted."

"Oh, don't say that." She felt a tremor of revulsion as he laid his sweating cheek against hers.

"No, it's true," he said. "So I . . . rejected God then. And now you're my God."

"Don't say things like that, that's blasphemy," she said, moving her face away from that sweating cheek, but having to hold on to him, for he seemed about to slip down between her arms.

"No, it's true. And I made the same mistake with you." Tears came into his drugged eyes.

"What mistake? No, go on, tell me," she said, for Earl had said to keep him talking no matter what.

"Same mistake. Trying to get too close. Gods are like the sun. You can't get too close. They'll burn you. Gods don't like you to get cheeky." Tears ran down his face but, incongruously, he was smiling. "It's cheeky, it's bad form to say, 'I love you. Let me serve you.' You may not be wanted. You may not be good enough."

"But I remember in school," she said. "The nuns said that God will always forgive you as long as you repent."

"No, no, you're not listening. I was cheeky with *you.* Offering my devotion, when all it did was make you want to go away and never see me again. You won't forgive me for offering my devotion, will you?"

"Bernard," she said. "Bernard, listen to me, never mind all that. You mightn't have much time. Won't you do this one thing for me and make your confession to a priest?"

"I . . . I don't need a priest . . ." Again he smiled horribly, while his eyes wept tears. "I'm making my confession to you."

"Okay, then," Earl said. He had come up behind them, and now he took Bernard firmly by the arm. "Let's walk a bit. Okay, Bernard?"

"Take your bloody paws off me," Bernard said. He swung around and threw a punch, but Earl moved his head aside with the practice of a fighter.

"Eileen," Earl said. "Let's walk him to the window and back. Walk and back. Come on, Bernard. You're going to die, man."

"Let me alone," Bernard said.

But it was Eileen who pulled him forward, her grip urgent. He's going to die. The day of Mama's first attack she had been there when Mama nearly died, Mama didn't want to die, she fought for her life. And this silly, bloody man was killing himself. She urged him forward. There was a knock on the door and Earl, letting go of Bernard, went to answer. The waiter, bringing in two pots of coffee, looked strangely at Bernard as Earl paid the bill. When the waiter had gone, Earl took over, walking Bernard up and down while she poured a cup of coffee. "Please, Bernard," she said. "Drink this for me. Please?"

He shook his head. "Look," she said. "You've been saying you'd do anything for me, but now you're doing something terrible, something I don't want you to do. And you're doing it, not for me, but for yourself. You talk about loving me, but when I ask you to do this one thing you don't want to do, you become like some wee spoiled boy."

As she said it, she saw him stare back at her, his eyes momentarily more clear than they had been. It was as though her contempt had shaken him awake, and for a moment, he was the old Bernard, clever and wanting to please her. "Do you know, you might be right," he said, as though surprised. He took the coffee cup and drank. "I didn't mean to hurt you. But you have a point. Yes, in a way, you might be right."

"Good," Earl said. "Keep walking, okay? We'll get you out of this."

"Now, Bernard," she said, handing him the refilled cup. "Take a sip of that, go on, drink up." He obeyed her. "Now, take my arm and we'll walk." She turned to Earl. "Did you get the doctor?"

"He's on his way."

"A doctor?" Bernard said. "What doctor?" He opened

his mouth as if to continue but seemed to have lost the thought. "All right," he said. "If it makes you happy."

"Keep walking," Earl said. "That will make her happy."

And so when he had finished the coffee they began to walk him again, moving past the Simmondses' stacked suitcases, past the baby's cot to the opened window, and back again to the bed. At the fourth circuit, Bernard's legs began to fail him and he staggered and tripped. Earl caught him and steadied him. "Keep moving," Earl told him. "And talk about something. Talk, you two." But when Eileen tried to think of something to say she could not, and besides, Bernard was becoming worse. His eyes seemed unable to stay open and his sweating face was now the color of cheap white soap. His feet dragged across the carpet like the steps of an old, old man. "Talk to me, then," Earl said. "How many pills did you take? Did you ever try this before? Say something."

"Ahhhh," Bernard said in a sort of moan that frightened Eileen. He slipped through her grip, half falling to his knees. Earl let go of his other arm and he pitched over as though unconscious. Earl bent down, caught him under the armpits, and dragged him up. "Take his legs," he said and together they lifted him onto the bed. "What will we do now?" she asked.

"Not much we can do. They're sending an ambulance." Earl lifted Bernard off the pillows and slapped his face. "Bernard, wake up!" But Bernard did not wake and, released, fell back lax on the pillows, his thin hair wet and disarranged. Eileen thought of a sea bird, dead and bedraggled on some beach, and at that moment, looking at him, she believed he had died. But then she saw a little pulse beating in his neck and ran to the table to pour coffee. "Maybe if we can get him to drink

[161]

this? Or, maybe, make him vomit? What did the doctor say, was it Dr. Irwin himself?"

"Yes. Oh, by the way, he said to tell you to tell Mona to go directly to St. Dunstan's Hospital, the intensive-care unit, and he'd meet her there."

"But she's not here," Eileen said.

"His wife?"

"Yes."

Just then there was a knock on the door. Earl opened. The assistant hotel manager came in, followed by two stretcher men.

"What happened?" the manager asked. "Did he take pills?"

Earl nodded. The stretcher men went to the bed, looked at Bernard, then lifted him off the bed and onto a stretcher, tucking him in with blankets.

"Is he very bad?" Eileen asked.

"Don't know yet, miss. Ready, Mike?"

"If you don't mind, I'd like you to use the service lift," the manager said. "It's by the back stairs. I'll show you the way."

"Right, then," the stretcher man said. They lifted Bernard up.

"Will we be able to see him?" Eileen asked.

"I don't know. If he's an overdose case, I imagine he won't be feeling much like having visitors for a while," the stretcher man said. They went out, followed by the manager, and Eileen went with them as far as the door, looking down at the stretcher, at Bernard's pale face, the sweating soapy skin, the untidy fringe of hair. It was as though she and Bernard had been in an accident and she had been the driver and he was the one who was hurt and was going to die. And it was her fault, although it was an accident.

When they had gone, Earl went to the bed table and

poured himself the rest of the wine. "Hungry?" he asked.

"No."

"Sandwich, maybe?"

"No, I couldn't. Do you think he'll die?"

"I don't know. I've seen people OD and come out of it, but I haven't known anybody who took that much sodium Amytal."

"I'd better go downstairs and write a note for Mona and put it in her box in case she comes in."

"Okay," Earl said. "I'll be here."

She went to him and kissed him. "Thank God, you *were* here," she said.

When she went downstairs the lobby was deserted except for a desk clerk, a porter dozing on the bench, and an old lady sitting in an armchair under the hall clock. Even the lounge seemed half empty with only one waiter serving half a dozen people at the tables by the bar. She went to the writing room to get writing paper, and as she did the revolving doors of the lobby entrance spun swiftly and several people entered from the street. Among them she noticed the young man she had seen Mona pick up in the lounge two days ago. He walked past her as though he were looking for somebody and went into the lounge where he stood peering about, then sat down at a table and signaled to the waiter. She went on to the writing room, where she found paper and envelopes but no pen. She went back to the lobby and asked the desk clerk if he could lend her a pen for a few minutes. As she did, she saw that there was a long, white envelope in her box.

"Is that for me?"

"Are you Miss Hughes?"

"Yes."

He gave her the envelope. It had her name on it: Miss

E. Hughes. She recognized Bernard's writing. Inside, she found her return airline ticket and three twenty-pound notes. He must have put this in her box before he went up to his suite to take the pills.

"Here we are, miss," the desk clerk said. "The pen you wanted."

She went into the lounge and sat down with pen and paper. She felt like crying, but the marijuana had dulled her. It was like an aspirin against grief. She took up the pen and wrote:

Dear Mona,
Bernard has been taken ill and is in the intensive-care unit in a hospital called St. Dunstan's. Dr. Irwin told me to tell you he will meet you there. But, please, when you get this, ring me. I will be in room 402 or in my own room.

Eileen

She wrote Mona's name on the envelope and took it back to the desk. "Will you put this in Mrs. McAuley's box? It's very urgent. Her husband has been taken to the hospital so I want to be sure she gets it the minute she comes in."

"Very good, miss."

There was a waiter standing near the desk, and as she started to leave he said to her, "Was it Mrs. McAuley you were asking about, miss?"

"Yes, that's right."

"She's in the dining room. Just came in a little while ago. She's having dinner."

"Oh, thank you." She turned and went along the corridor to the dining room, which was in the rear of the hotel. It was a big cold room with dark mahogany furniture, white tablecloths, and unpleasantly bright electric lights. It was a place where people staying at the hotel ate early and often alone, and as Eileen came toward it she saw that it was almost empty, that many of the tables had been reset for breakfast, and that the waiters stood in a group, chatting, like workers waiting for a factory bell. When she saw Mona sitting alone at a small table in the center of the room, it was as though Mona was a woman in a painting, a painting of loneliness, the almost empty dining room, the waiters bored, waiting to go home, the woman alone, dressed for the evening, a half bottle of wine and a half-eaten meal in front of her, reading a paperback book she had propped up against a cruet stand. Mona, who had probably been off hunting men and now had come back hungry from her roamings, to read some book as she dined alone. But what book could equal the drama of her own life this night? And then Eileen remembered that Mona did not yet know the news.

An old headwaiter came up. "Yes, miss?"

"I'm just—thanks, I'm with that lady over there."

"I'm afraid the kitchen is closed now, miss."

"That's all right," she said, confused, and went past him, going toward Mona's table. Mona did not look up but went on reading, even when Eileen reached her table. And when she did look up, Eileen saw in her eyes the dulled, slightly distracted look of a person who has had too much to drink.

"Oh, it's you," Mona said. "Where did you spring from? Have you had your supper?"

She sat on the chair opposite Mona's. "Mona, Bernard is ill. He's been taken to hospital."

Mona's face sagged in alarm. "What's the matter with him?"

"He took an overdose of sleeping pills. They've taken him to the intensive-care unit in St. Dunstan's Hospital. Dr. Irwin said for me to tell you to meet him there."

"But I've been here nearly an hour," Mona said belligerently.

"I didn't know that. I put a note in your box just now. I'm baby-sitting upstairs."

"Baby-sitting? What's going on? St. Dunstan's, did you say?" Mona rose with a lurch, almost upsetting her meal as she bumped clumsily against the table's edge. "Is he bad? When did it happen?"

"About an hour ago. The ambulance man said we probably won't be able to see him for a while."

"You're not seeing him," Mona said. "He's seen enough of you. You go to hell."

She spoke in a loud voice, loud enough for the few other diners to hear, and they did. She hurried to the dining-room door, a waiter coming after her, asking if everything was all right. She did not answer the waiter but as Eileen followed her out, she saw Mona break into a stumbling run, her half-drunken face looking as though it would collapse into weeping. In the lobby Mona said in a loud voice, "Get a taxi, please, porter, it's an emergency!" and at the sound of her loud voice Eileen saw the young man sitting in the lounge look up, recognize Mona, then run out into the lobby in pursuit of her.

"Hello, there," he called, a grin on his face. "How are you?"

Mona turned to see who had spoken, her drink-flushed face blank as she looked at him.

"I came here on the off chance I'd run into you," he said. "How are things?"

"Go away," Eileen heard Mona say. "Leave me alone, for God's sake. My husband's been taken sick." And turned from him, pushing out of the revolving doors, going into the street, leaving the young man staring after her, leaving Eileen too, uncertain what to do next, wanting to go to the hospital but remembering the baby upstairs. It was the sort of night there was no luck around. What if Earl took more marijuana and fell asleep and something went wrong with the baby. Again, she would be responsible. She took the lift up to the Simmondses' room.

"Hi," Earl said, letting her in. "You all right?"

"Yes. I just met his wife and told her."

"And I heard from Arlene," he said. "She called from the theater to say they'll be home in half an hour. Do you want to go over to the hospital? I'll look after the baby."

"Did you tell her what happened? I mean, Arlene."

"No, that's too much of a hassle. I just said everything's fine and we'd see her later. So you go ahead. I'll come over in a while and see how you're getting on."

She looked at the baby. It was asleep. "Well, I will go, then," she said, deciding. "If that's all right with you?"

He smiled at her, and in that familiar, easy way of his, he took her in his arms and kissed her. And she clung to him, she who had not yet had a real boy friend, who had never been in love, who was waiting for all these things to happen to her as they were supposed to happen to girls her age. Not like tonight, not the likes of Bernard McAuley trying to kill himself because of her, not even this strange and exciting thing that had happened with Earl, for she did not know Earl, he took drugs, and if it hadn't been for the drugs, she thought that none of it might have happened. Not this, not this stranger, even though he was handsome and kind and warm, but something more ordinary, some boy she would meet in a normal way, some boy who would love her and let her love him, too.

Gently, Earl ended the kiss. "Off you go. Maybe I'll see you later."

And then she was alone in the corridor, going to the lift. Alone.

The intensive-care unit was on the ground floor of the hospital, sealed off at the end of a long corridor by a door marked NO ADMITTANCE. The corridor walls were of bright-green tile, lit by harsh electric lights which produced the tense atmosphere of an operating room. "Are you a relative?" a nurse asked, peering out from behind the No Admittance door. The nurse was young and black and spoke in a West Indian accent.

"Yes, I'm his wife. I'm supposed to see Dr. Irwin."

"Dr. Irwin. Just take a seat please. I'll find out."

The door swung shut. Mona sat on the corridor bench next to an old man who was bundled up in a greasy sheepskin-lined overcoat and a woolen muffler, although it was summer. He smelled of whiskey. "Do you have somebody in here?" he asked at once.

"Yes. My husband."

"I have a daughter. Those bloody drugs. It's not the first time I've had to bring her in here and it won't be the last, I warrant you." He relapsed into silence and scuffed his worn suede boots against each other. Mona began to pray. She did not know why but she started an act of contrition. Oh, my God, I am heartily sorry for all my sins because they are displeasing to Thee Who art so deserving of all my love, and I firmly resolve by the help of Thy holy grace never more to offend Thee and to amend my life. It was as though she tried to make a covenant with God, offering to amend her life in exchange for Bernard's life. For now, faced by that shut door, she felt a terror of his dying, a feeling that he would die now without her ever knowing the truth of what had gone wrong. The things she had wondered about over the last four years and given up as insoluble riddles came back to her. Why did he wait until he was thirty before he married? Her own father had married late, Irishmen often did, but knowing Bernard and the chances his money gave him with all sorts of girls, why had he not married sooner? And why did he not want children? And why after courting her and marrying her and making love to her like a man possessed nearly every night for the first three months, did he make love hardly at all for the next three months, and, after that, never? What was the matter with him? It wasn't that he had taken up with someone else, for he had never looked at another girl until Eileen. And he and Eileen were not lovers. And he'd said he never wanted that. If you could believe him. If you ever knew what really went on in that head of his. The only time they had discussed sex, the only time he would discuss it, was that first year, that time she burst into tears and asked him what was wrong with her that he no longer slept with her. He said it wasn't her fault at all. He said he had found out that he just couldn't stand being dependent on another person's body. He said he was sorry, but that he knew now that love had nothing to do with sex. Sex was just an urge, it was like relieving yourself, and you might as well do it on your own. She knew what he was talking about by then, she had seen the books and pictures in his study, but at the time she was shy about mentioning it to him. She thought he would get over it. But even though she did her best, parading herself naked or half dressed in front of him, and making up to him in bed to try to give him a hard-on, it was no use. He didn't want it. He began to shut himself away in his study until all hours, reading about art and history, and then it was classical music, thousands of pounds spent on turntables and speakers which, a few months later, lay covered and unused. And then it was the plays he produced for the Liskean Players and after that they went to Europe, and then it was the building sites that took all his attention, and then it was giving big parties for people he didn't even care about. And none of it helped. It wasn't her fault: he was right about that. He was all alone and she couldn't help him and he didn't even want her trying. Until Eileen.

And now, because of Eileen, he was going to die. She stared at the shut door. Oh, God, please, God, don't let him die.

For, if he did, she did not know what she would do. She would be well looked after, she was sure of that. She could probably keep the big shop going and sell off the other businesses, but it would not be the same without him. Odd and all as he was, strange as their life had been together, she could not think of losing him. Bernard. Oh, Bernard. He might not be able to hear her anymore, even if she shouted out his name in a scream in this corridor. He might be in there, dead. The last dead person she had seen was her father. She had come home from Dublin, where she was training as a chemist, to find that the funeral was already arranged and that neighbors had laid her father out in the poky wee flat over what was his dental surgery in Kent Street. She remembered somebody had wrapped rosary beads around her father's fingers, fingers that she had never seen holding a rosary in his life. She remembered his soft white hands, hands eager to get into his patients' mouths and probe for tender gums, wandering hands that bothered women and had to be slapped away, hands that money slid through, which was one of the reasons she had been grateful to Bernard, for money stuck to his. Her father, who was so different from Bernard, who blamed everybody else for his troubles, who always smelled of ether and cigarettes, and often sat all afternoon in his dental chair, reading old magazines, waiting, in case some patient might walk in off the street. Not enough did. She never knew why. Other dentists seemed to do all right, but her father had always been out of step, her father, who parted his wavy hair in the middle and grew a Clark Gable mustache long after it was out of fashion, who hung around the golf club bar when he hadn't paid his dues and had to be asked not to come back. Her father, who lived all his life always a bit short, who said himself he was "catching the divil by the coattails." Who was the opposite of Bernard in every way.

She looked at the No Admittance door. Was Derek Irwin in there or not? What was keeping him? Was it because they were working on Bernard now, pumping out his stomach, or what? Was he dead? Oh, God, please, God, spare him. I didn't start this. Two days after I took her on, he went into the shop and saw her, and when he came home that night he was changed: it started right then, the first time he ever laid eyes on her, he began ordering me around like an employee. At dinner that night he suddenly said: "What do you think of that new girl, Eileen Hughes?" And I said: "She's all right. I suppose she'll do." And he said: "Do? I think she'll be very good. Very good. I want you to promote her and encourage her." And that was so unlike him that I said: "So that's what you fancy now. Tall skinny kids." And he said, "What would you know about it? What do you know about looks? The trouble with you is, you can't see beyond a pretty face because that's your purse. There are some things you'd never understand." And when I asked him what exactly it was that I'd never understand, he got up and left the room. What I didn't understand was why he would say such a mean thing about my pretty face being my purse; if he meant by that that I married him just for his money, he was dead wrong, I married him because I liked him, but that's men all over, twisting things around to suit themselves. He was the one who was mercenary, always driving me up to Dublin to expensive restaurants and ordering champagne at dances and implying that there'd be plenty more of the same if only I'd marry him. But I married him because he was clever and I liked him. I still do. And he was the one who started me with men. I never did a thing until that second year we were married when I met Tom Dempsey. Now *he* was really good-looking, he was doing a *locum* for Dr. McCall, who was on his holidays, and it was hot and heavy for a while, the two of us in Tom's car on the back roads outside Lismore and meeting up in Belfast in the afternoons. All right, I suppose it wasn't Bernard started me on that, but when he did find out about me and Tom, would anyone believe what he said to me. "Look," he said. "Some of this is my fault for not paying more attention to you. But I can't have you doing the likes of that around home. If you do it again, I'll divorce you. But we're grown up, both of us. When we go to London or Paris, you can do what you want while you're there, just as long as it's nobody we know and nobody who knows people at home. You can go off on holidays on your own, too. Is that fair enough?"

Well, that wasn't a very Irish arrangement, was it? I remember I didn't believe one word of it. And the first time we went to London after that, I decided to call his bluff. So, just for badness, I told him I'd met somebody and would like to use the suite that afternoon, if he didn't mind. And all he said was: "How long will you need it for? I can stay out all night, if you like." And that was long before he met Eileen, so it wasn't just meeting Eileen that changed him. Who knows why he does anything? When I think he's in there, maybe dying, and I still don't know what makes him tick. Well, I do know a bit more about him since Eileen. I know that whatever he's looking for in his life, Eileen has come the closest to being it. And who'd believe that from the very beginning he's not said a word to her? Oh, he's the queer one, from the very first he hid it from her, although he always managed to drop in at the shop in the afternoons, and usually he'd have a casual word with her; she had no idea, I know, for when he started disappearing on weekends, wasn't I the one who used to be skulking about, hiding in doorways, spying on her when she went in and out of her house in Church Street? And I was the one who hunted the back roads on Sundays, the same back roads Tom Dempsey and I used, looking for Bernard's car and expecting to find the pair of them in it. But I found nothing. I think the truth was, he sneaked out on weekends to wander around the town, hoping to get a glimpse of her in the streets. I think it, but I don't know it. All I know is, there was nothing going on. The time I went to Brussels on my own, after he wouldn't come to London with me, I had a great time, but I cut it short because I was suddenly sure he had refused to come because he was going to see Eileen. And so I flew home on a Saturday night, thinking to catch them. But he was up at a building site and she was working overtime in the shop. And then there was the row about him sending flowers and chocolates to her mother, that first time in the hospital. When I found out, I warned him, I said: "Bernard, don't be cross with me now, but if you start doing the like of that, we're in for trouble. You know what this town is like." We were getting ready for bed at the time and he said: "You don't have to worry. She'll never know. Nobody will know. I don't ever want her to know." And I said: "Ah, but sooner or later you're bound to let something slip, sooner or later you'll make a fool of yourself over this girl." I thought he'd strike me, but instead he said: "Mona, don't be against me," and I saw that look on his face, that look I've seen since, as if I had a gun and I was going to shoot him. "Oh, Mona," he said.

There are a lot of things you like about your life, isn't that true? So why spoil everything? Look, we've sent flowers to employees and their families before when someone was sick. And I sent it in both our names. Trust me. I'll be very careful. I have no intention of ever letting her know. That's the only way, the pure way, the one way I can continue to be happy. But I need your help. If you help me everything will be all right. But if you don't it will all be spoiled and then I don't know what I'd do. I don't know what I'd do, do you hear? But if you help me now, I promise I'll make it up to you. Please?" He was trembling when he said it. I declare to God, he looked like a man who'd been condemned to death. "Help you?" I said. "It's God help you, I think." But that was the night I decided I had to help him, that was the night I made up my mind. The next day neither one of us spoke about it, but a week later I gave Eileen a rise in pay and put her in charge of cosmetics and told her if she did well there I might move her up in charge of junior fashions. And after that paid for her to take a training course in selling in Belfast two afternoons a week. And when we gave big parties at our house, I'd ask her. Of course people thought it was me who was making a pet of her, and of course there were ones in the shop who resented her. Nobody ever guessed about Bernard, nobody. And then I took her to Dublin with us because, anyway, Dublin was off limits for men and I knew I'd have plenty of men this summer when we came to London. But Dublin was my downfall, I see that now. Once he had her all to himself for three days without her getting suspicious, then there was no stopping him. That's when he must have decided to go behind my back and bring her to London without asking me. I suppose he thought if she was with us, there would be nothing for me to do but go along with it, back down, have a holiday the three of us, and no men. That's why he bought three tickets for everything here. Yes, it was Dublin that did us in, bringing her to Dublin that made him think of bringing her here, maybe even made him think of buying that huge house in Louth and having her come to live with us. I should have put my foot down the minute I found out about London, I could have stopped him dead by threatening to tell Eileen what was going on. But I was afraid of him, because I don't know him, I don't know what he might do. And now it's come to this, to this bright corridor, this waiting, to this not knowing if he's alive or dead. Oh, my God, I am heartily sorry, please spare him. Merciful Jesus, please spare him.

But as she began again to pray, starting to ask a God she never thought about anymore, beginning again the memorized words of the act of contrition, turning it into a covenant she offered to God, the No Admittance door opened and there was Derek Irwin, his purplish face grave, God's messenger, bringing her news of life or death, Derek Irwin, a Protestant with a posh accent that made her ill at ease, but still he came as though summoned by her prayer. She stood up, afraid.

"Hello, Mona."

"Hello, Derek, what's the news?"

He did not speak but glanced at the old man on the bench, then took her arm, walking her up the corridor as though preparing her for bad news. She felt herself tremble. God had refused her. She looked up into the purplish face of God's messenger. "Is he dead?"

"No, he's alive. He took a killing dose, though. It was lucky he was found. Another half hour and it would have been all over."

"Will he be all right, then?"

"I think so. They're dialyzing him now."

"Dialyzing? But isn't that what they do for kidney failure?"

"Yes, the same machine. They're using it to filter the barbiturates out of his system."

"And when will you know?"

"He'll be all right. It should take about twelve hours. The fellow I spoke to on the phone thinks he took about fifteen sodium Amytal. With an overdose like that he went into coma quite fast. It was lucky they found him, as I said."

"Who found him?" she asked, confused. "What fellow did you speak to on the phone?"

"An American. He rang me up. A friend of your friend, Eileen. They found him."

"But how did they know? Did he tell her he was doing it?"

"Don't ask me," Derek Irwin said. "Well, I'm sorry about this. Too bad about your holiday. They'll have to keep him in hospital for several days."

"When can I see him?"

"He's still in coma. He should come out of it in an hour or two. They might let you in for a few minutes then. You could ring up and ask."

"Oh, I'm not going to leave here."

"Well, as you like. I'll look in on him tomorrow morning. Do you have my home phone number?"

"No."

"Here's my card. I'll ask Betty to give you a ring tomorrow. Now, not to worry, he's in the best place. They're first-rate here."

"Thanks, Derek."

"You know that we saw him yesterday," Derek said. "He seemed in good form. You never know with people. He got the prescription from me, damnit. Said he was having trouble sleeping. Has he been depressed lately?"

She looked at him. Nobody must know, nobody must

know any of this. "No," she said. "He hasn't, really. And, by the way, I hope we'll be able to keep this to ourselves. You know what it's like in Ireland, especially when it's someone like Bernard, who has a lot of business connections. It would do him harm."

"Oh, don't worry, we won't, of course, say a word. But, mind you, he's going to need help. Psychiatric counseling of some sort. They'll talk to you about that here, after he's a bit better. Find out what's upsetting him and so forth. They'll want to make sure there's no recurrence of what upset him in the first place. Anyway, not to worry for now. Good night. I'll talk to you tomorrow."

She watched him go off down the bright-lit corridor, watched him go from big to small, a distant, tiny figure disappearing around a corner. She turned and went back to the bench. "Was that your doctor?" the old man asked.

"Yes."

"Good news, was it?"

"Yes."

He nodded and scuffed his worn suede boots, rubbing their heels against each other. "That's good, then," he said and seemed to draw his head in like a turtle, hunching up the collar of his sheepskin coat. She sat beside him and looked again at the door marked No Admittance. Behind that door he was lying, hooked up to a machine that was filtering poison out of his blood, poison he had taken because he was mad in love with a stupid girl who didn't even know it. Poor bloody Bernard. And now I'll have to keep on the right side of her, I'll have to make sure she keeps her mouth shut. It was a mistake to have been cross with her tonight. Maybe I should ring the hotel and tell her what's happening.

But she did not want to go away and look for a telephone in case the nurse came out and said she could see

Bernard. And so she sat there and after a few minutes heard footsteps in the corridor and, looking up, saw, coming toward her, the tall, slender figure of Eileen Hughes, the new bad angel in their lives, the new third partner in their marriage. And knew then that to have agreed for his sake to be nice to this girl was like a mortal sin, a sin that once you had committed it, there was no going back on. For now she needed Eileen Hughes as never before. This girl, in her innocence and her ignorance, must become part of a pact, a pact among the three of them to conceal all that had happened tonight. And so she stood up and went forward along the corridor with a smile on her lips, a smile she carried like a rifle, advancing across no-man's-land to confront her enemy.

When Eileen saw that Mona was smiling, her heart lifted. He was still alive.

"Hello, Mona, how is he? I'm sorry, I know you don't want me here, but I was so worried."

Mona at once shook her head as though negating her former anger. She took Eileen by the arm in the manner of Dr. Irwin and, as he had done, walked down the corridor to tell the news. "It's bad," she said. "But they say he has a good chance now. Of course, he's still in a coma."

"Have you seen him?"

"No, not yet." And she told Eileen about the machine that would take twelve hours to filter his blood and how he would have to stay in hospital for several days. She said this in a low, confiding tone, friendly, but concerned, as though she had completely forgotten the angry words she had spoken earlier, as though Eileen were a close relative on whom she could lean, someone who would do whatever was possible to help in this hour of near-tragedy. And Eileen, grateful to be treated in this way, having expected to face more of Mona's rudeness, at once assumed the role assigned her. They walked back to sit on the bench outside the No Admittance door, talking in low tones as though they were in church. "We're going to have our work cut out for us," Mona said. "The doctor says it will be very hard for him."

"What do you mean, Mona?"

"Well, it seems they're very depressed afterward and there's always the danger that they'll try again and the doctor said I must be sure and see he's not worried about anything. Of course, you're going to be a big part of it."

"Me?"

"Yes, I'm going to need your help. We'll talk about that later. I was thinking of taking him away someplace for a while, maybe for a month or so. There's a hotel down in Connemara we used to stay at years ago. It's nice and quiet and in the country. If I can get him to go, that is."

"It sounds like a good idea," Eileen said.

"Of course, the first thing that would upset him now is if he thought this would come out and people would know about it. You see that, of course."

"Yes, of course."

"I mean, Bernard's always hated to be sick, he hates letting on to anyone that there's anything wrong with him. Apart from that, you know what people are like, they'd be saying he was around the bend and that would affect his business. And he's easily hurt, as you know."

"I know."

"So"—and here Mona put her hand on Eileen's sleeve—"I just hope I can count on you. I don't think this is anybody's business but the three of us. Don't you agree?"

"Yes, I do."

[179]

"I know it's awkward for you, it's only natural that you'd tell your mother about this. But we'd be very grateful to you, both Bernard and myself, if you wouldn't mention any of this, even to your mother. I know I've no real right to ask you that."

"No, that's all right. I won't tell her."

"I think that's wise. Apart from anything else, it might worry her and her not well."

"I know."

"Thanks, Eileen, thanks very much." Mona leaned toward Eileen and gave her a sort of embrace. "God," she said. "Who would ever have thought it would come to this. I never thought he would do something like this, did you?"

"Oh, I don't know him," Eileen said. "I had no notion that anything was wrong until the other day. You know he never said a word to me back at home. That's true, Mona."

"I know." Mona nodded. "I blame myself. I do. I should have said something. But I thought it was some silly crush he'd get over in a month or two."

"But it is. It is."

"But will he?" Mona said. "That's the big question."

"He's got to. I mean, one thing I think I should do, if I can manage it, is to leave Lismore and get a job someplace else, someplace where there'll be no chance of running into him."

"That's not going to be easy, with your mother needing you. Anyway, it's too soon to talk about that."

"How long do you think he'll be in the hospital?"

"I don't know. I want to get him home to Ireland as soon as he's fit to travel."

Eileen was going to ask if Mona wanted her to go on home tomorrow if she could get a flight out, or would she like her to stay on at least till Sunday. But then she saw, coming along the corridor, the jaunty figure of

Earl, moving with his wobbly, high-heeled, cowboy walk. She saw Mona look up at the sight of him, handsome and strange in his fringed shirt, with his long hair and mustache. "Mona," she said, in a low, confiding voice, "this fellow coming now is Earl, he's an American. He's the person who phoned Dr. Irwin and helped get Bernard into the hospital."

"But who is he?"

"He's a friend of the people I was baby-sitting for."

"Hi, there," Earl said. He smiled at Eileen and then at Mona. "You're Mrs. McAuley, right?"

"Yes." Eileen could see that, no matter what had happened, Mona was Mona, she reacted to a good-looking boy.

"How's it going now?"

"Better. They have him on a dialysis machine."

"Good," Earl said. He sat down beside Mona as though he were an old, old friend. "Then he should be okay."

"The doctor said he has a very good chance." Mona looked at Earl as she said this. "I hear I have you to thank for getting him to hospital."

"Eileen is the one to thank," Earl said, and smiled at Eileen. "Hey, kid, what about some coffee? We can bring some back for Mrs. McAuley."

"Mona."

"Mona." Earl smiled at her. "And don't worry. Everything is okay now. Eileen?"

Earl was waiting for her, waiting to get her off on her own, Earl who had just been in bed with her, the first boy ever. But she didn't feel she should go with him, not now, not when all this was going on. She should stay with Mona.

"You go ahead, then," Mona said. "I'll have milk, no sugar. Or, better, tea with milk, if they have it."

"Gotcha," Earl said. He rose and put out his hand and took Eileen's hand and raised her to her feet, smiling at her, possessive yet gentle. She went with him, although she worried about it, worried about walking out on Mona. What had happened tonight had made Mona a different person, somebody you could be sorry for, not like the old Mona.

"Are you okay?" Earl asked, as they walked off down the corridor.

"Yes. Did Arlene and Bill come back?"

"Yes, they said to thank you. I told them you had to go early, a friend was ill in hospital."

"You didn't need to come," she said. "It was nice of you, though."

"My pleasure." He smiled at her in his distant, happy way, and suddenly with a sad feeling, she realized that he was quite drunk. She wondered if he was one of those drunk persons who would not remember all this when he woke tomorrow. "Anyway," he said, "I'm hungry. Let's go eat something. Ice cream. I always get this craze for ice cream when I'm stoned. Yeah, but they don't make good ice cream in England. You hungry, kid?"

"No," she said. "No, I'd better get some coffee and bring it back to Mona."

"Okay, let's get coffee. And let's take off."

"Well, we'll see."

Then a nurse came by and Earl asked her where they could get coffee and the nurse said there was no place they could get it now. The hospital café was shut and there was no place around here, the nurse said. She spoke to Earl with the coldness some people showed toward Americans, but he did not seem to notice. Then, when the nurse had moved on, he said, "This country runs on one cylinder. Why can't they stay open, for Christ's sake?" He seemed as though he was about to be angry, as a drunk person gets angry, but nothing came of it, for when she looked at him worriedly, he at once smiled his distant smile. "Let's go outside for a moment. Let's go out in the yard and smoke a joint."

"Oh, you go. I'd better go back to Mona. She'd probably be glad of some company."

He looked at her, cocking his head to one side. She noticed that he had a little trouble focusing on her. "What are you, a professional baby sitter?" he said. "Listen, the guy who OD'd is going to be out for a while. There's nothing you can do for him, nothing she can do for him. So why not let's you and I smoke a little grass, so you can get your high back. Then we'll go eat some ice cream and talk about Paris, or something."

But she did not want to go and smoke marijuana in some hospital yard, or watch him smoke it either. She wished he were more as he had been earlier, responsible, gentle, a person she depended on. "You go ahead," she said. "Please, I don't want any more."

"Okay, then. We'll go back to Mona." He took her by the arm. "Let's go."

"You don't have to come back with me," she said, feeling awkward and wrong.

"I know that," he said, and again his smile was distant, his manner calm. "Let's go." He turned her toward the intensive-care unit. As they came into the corridor, she saw Mona sitting talking to the old man on the bench, and as they came closer the old man stood up, said goodbye to Mona, and passed them, giving them an inquisitive look. Earl went up to Mona and said, "Sorry, there's no coffee. Maybe we can go out and find some. Want to come with us?"

"No, I'd better stay here."

"Well, in that case I'll take Eileen off and feed her. She hasn't had supper. That okay with you?"

"Yes, of course," Mona said. She seemed confused by Earl. "You go ahead," she said to Eileen.

"No, no," Eileen said quickly, narrowing her eyes at Mona to warn her she didn't really want to go with Earl. She turned to Earl and said, "Look, thanks very much, Earl, but I think it would be better if I stayed here with Mona. You go ahead and get your ice cream, or whatever."

He stood, rocked back on his wobbly heels, staring at her quizzically, a gunfighter who might draw or back off from the encounter. "I just want to have a smoke. And some ice cream. Don't you want to come? What's the matter, am I out of favor or something?"

She felt herself blush, felt Mona's eyes on her, saw that Earl might just turn cross, you never knew, especially with someone on drugs. "No," she said. "No, of course not, Earl. I'd just better stay, that's all. And thanks. Thanks very much for coming."

"So," he said. He rocked on his heels and suddenly sang out: "So, it's goodbye-ee," his voice loud as a drunk's in the silent corridor. "Good night, sweetheart, good night!" He stopped singing and looked at her soulfully. "Does this mean we're never going to see each other again?"

She grinned at him, embarrassed, aware that Mona was taking all this in. "That depends," she said. "If you come to Ireland, look me up."

"A sweet kid," he said, smiling his warm smile. He turned to Mona. "Isn't she a sweet kid?"

Mona nodded politely. "Yes, she is."

"And you," Earl looked at Mona with mock intensity. "You are beautiful. Beautiful." And in the gentle, assured way he had had with Eileen, he put out his hands, took Mona by the hands, and raised her off the bench. He took her in his arms and kissed her. "Good luck," he said.

He released her, then turned to Eileen with the self-same warm smile. He took Eileen in his arms. "My favorite baby sitter," he said. "Goodbye, my love." And kissed her, not as he had kissed her before, but a kiss of benediction on the brow, releasing her.

He backed off then, from both of them, retreating up the corridor, waving at them like someone saying goodbye in a film. "*Adios!*" he called out, then turned away, and Eileen watched him go, heartsick, yet not wanting to follow him: watched his happy, wobbly walk until he turned the corner and disappeared.

They sat, Mona and she, in a moment of silence.

"Who on earth is he, that fellow?" Mona wondered.

"He works for a record company," Eileen said dully. She felt she was going to cry.

"He's well on, I'd say."

"No, it's marijuana mostly. He's been smoking it all evening."

"Oh, so that explains it," Mona said. "He seemed a nice sort of fellow, though."

"Yes. He was a big help with the doctor."

"I should have thanked him properly," Mona began and was going to say something else when the No Admittance door opened and a nurse came out.

"Mrs. McAuley?"

"Yes, Nurse."

"You can come in now, for a minute. But only for a minute."

Mona rose without looking at Eileen and followed the nurse inside as though she were being summoned to judgment. She went into a small shut world of machines, of screens monitoring heartbeats, of plastic bottles dripping plasma, of patients lying still as corpses or thrashing in pain. She saw all of this yet did not see it, for it was as though her vision blurred until the nurse took her through a larger room into one of the small rooms

[185]

at the side, a room in which there were two patients, each hooked up to a bedside dialysis machine, patients whose heartbeats danced on screens above their heads, Bernard in one bed and a young girl in the other. The girl was awake: her eyes were open. A nurse stood over Bernard, taking his pulse, obscuring Mona's view of his face. The nurse who had brought her in whispered: "He's just become conscious. Now, you're only to stay for a minute, please." She nodded, and Mona nodded to show she had understood. The nurse went out.

There was no place to sit. Mona, standing submissively behind the pulse-taking nurse, looked over at the other bed. The girl in it was young and rosy-cheeked and now had closed her eyes and seemed to be asleep. Was she the daughter of that old man in the sheepskin coat? Just then the pulse-taking nurse finished with Bernard and moved across the room to take the girl's pulse. Mona could at last see Bernard. For a second she thought they had made a mistake: it was not Bernard. The face that was on the pillow was gap-toothed, the eyes seemed unfocused. It was the face of an idiot. When Bernard was a boy he had fallen off a horse and broken several front teeth. He was secretive about it, and although he wore both upper and lower bridges he pretended that he had no false teeth. In the four years of their marriage Mona had only seen him once without them when she came into the bathroom without his knowing it. But now she saw him defenseless, bare-gummed, looking like a beggar, his blind eyes not seeming to see her. Afraid, she wondered if the sleeping pills had impaired his mind. "Bernard," she whispered. "Bernard, it's me."

But the face on the pillow did not seem to hear. After a moment he uttered a gibbering moan that terrified her. "Bernard," she said loudly, bending over him. His eyes seemed to focus on her for a moment, his mouth worked as though he was trying to say something, but there was no sound. Suddenly she felt her eyes burn with tears. She reached out and took his face in her hands and put her cheek against his sweating cheek. The tears came then, just as she felt the nurse touch her shoulder. "Come now," the nurse said. "We have to work. And I'm afraid he'll not know you, not yet. Come."

But she held his face and kissed it, kissed his poor cheeks, his toothless mouth, until the nurse eased her away. As she went toward the door she kept looking back, hoping that he had known her, looked at his eyes, eyes which stared at her across that infinite gulf which had opened between them.

Friday, August 29

On Thursday night in the middle of the evening news the television set went on the blink; no picture, only sound. Agnes Hughes phoned McCusker's first thing on Friday morning, but they said they were sorry they could not send anyone before Saturday at the earliest and it would probably be Monday. So it would be Tuesday, knowing McCusker's. It was a nuisance being without the telly all weekend but she consoled herself that Eileen would be home on Sunday. All day yesterday she had been expecting her daughter to ring, but the phone had been silent. Maybe she would call this morning. The last time, Eileen had rung around 9 a.m. But the morning went on and Mrs. McTurk came and worked and talked and left, and then there was the long afternoon and still no ring. She wondered if Eileen had forgotten. She thought of ringing her, but what was the sense in that, let her have her holiday in peace, it's little enough time she gets off on her own without me to worry about.

At six o'clock the phone rang. "Mama?"

"Ah, there you are. How are you getting on?"

"I'm in Belfast."

"In Belfast? What happened?"

"Bernard got sick. I'll tell you all about it when I get home. I'm just taking the bus now, it's leaving in about five minutes so I should be home around eight."

The bus, Agnes Hughes thought, so she's on her own. "Bernard and Mona aren't with you, then?"

"No, they're still in London. He's in the hospital."

"What's the matter with him?"

"I'll tell you when I get home. It's all right, it's not serious. I must go now."

"I'll have supper ready for you."

"Don't bother, I'm all right."

But it gave her something to do. She had mincemeat in the house and had been going to use it for her dinner tomorrow. She decided to make a shepherd's pie, mince wasn't the best filling but it would do, and shepherd's pie was something Eileen liked. She also made a treacle cake, another thing Eileen sometimes asked for. As she worked around the kitchen she wondered what Bernard McAuley had, he was thin and young and healthy, he wasn't a drinker like his father had been. Of course, it could be something he had picked up in London. Still, wasn't it bad luck, and typical, for poor Eileen to be invited to London for a holiday, all expenses paid, and to have it cut short because the people who invited her got sick. Still, it's an ill wind. I'll be glad to have her home. I missed her.

It was half-eight when she heard Eileen's key in the front door. She came out of the kitchen into the hall, smiling, holding her arms out in welcome. But the moment Eileen kissed her and embraced her, she knew something was wrong. Eileen held on too long, as though she had run in from the street, afraid.

"Well, so what happened?"

Eileen took her suitcase in and put it at the foot of the stairs. "Bernard got food poisoning."

"And it's bad, is it?"

"He's in hospital, and they say he'll have to stay there for several days and take it easy when he gets home."

"And when did it happen?"

"Yesterday. I felt it was better I come home. I managed to get a flight this afternoon after hanging around the airport for hours. I'm dead."

"I have some supper for you, shepherd's pie and a pudding."

"Have you eaten yourself, yet?"

"No, not yet."

"Well, then. But I warn you, I'm not very hungry."

And so they went into the little breakfast nook off the kitchen and Eileen sat down while her mother went to the oven. "So it was something he ate, then?"

"Yes. He's in intensive care in the hospital. Or he was. He might be out of it by now."

"Intensive care? That's funny," Agnes Hughes said. "They don't usually put them in intensive care for the like of that."

"Well, I don't know. I never saw him," Eileen said, sounding cross, as though her word had been doubted. "Anyway, he's quite sick."

"Well, and apart from that, how did you enjoy London?"

"Oh, it was great. I loved it. I wish I could have seen more of it."

"I remember you said Mona was off on her own at the first? How did that work out, did she join you later in the week?"

"Yes. Yes, she came with us."

"Ah, she's a great girl. Wasn't it nice of her sending those lovely flowers and the chocolates for my birthday? Ah, it was rotten luck this happening on their holiday."

She put the pie on the table and cut the crust on the potato topping. It had come out quite nicely, but Eileen only picked at it. They talked a bit then, about the play Eileen had seen and about her having tea at the Ritz. It had been years since Agnes Hughes had been in London: it must have changed a lot. She had hoped that Eileen would get to see Hampton Court, and now she asked if she had.

"No. He only took me to one place and it wasn't very old, it was called Kenwood House."

"Was it nice?"

"Is that the phone?" Eileen said and got up, for it was. Who could it be at nine o'clock at night? She heard Eileen in the hall where the phone was. "Hello? Oh, it's you. Yes. I got a flight out at six. How is he? Is he off the machine yet? Oh, good. Yes, yes, I'm with her now. What? All right. You'll ring tomorrow, then. All right. Good night."

Eileen came into the kitchen. "Mama, that's Mona on the line. She'd like to say hello to you."

"And I'd like to speak to her," Agnes Hughes said, getting up in a rush.

"Now, take your time," Eileen warned, but she hurried all the same. It was a trunk call from London, after all.

"Hello, Mona," she said, feeling breathless as she spoke into the receiver. "I'm sorry about your news."

"Ah, yes, it's too bad. I don't know what he ate but whatever it was it's made him very sick."

"Eileen said he was in intensive care. It must have been serious."

"Oh, he was only in there for a few hours," Mona said. "Of course, I forgot, you were a nurse, weren't you?"

"I was."

"Then you probably know more about it than me. No, they were worried about him, but he's come out of it well. I have him in a private room now."

"I'm very sorry."

"Oh, well, these things happen. Anyway, what I wanted to speak to you about, Agnes, is that we feel badly, both of us, about Eileen's holiday."

"Oh, no, you shouldn't. Sure she's been telling me what a great time she had."

"Well, anyway," Mona McAuley said, "I've told her to take a week off work now and not to go into the shop until Bernard and I are home again. I'm hoping to bring him home by the end of next week. I want you to make sure she takes a little extra holiday. I know she's very conscientious, but I spoke to Bernard today and both of us want her to have next week off."

"Oh, that's very good of you. Very kind. I'll be glad to have her with me."

"Of course you will. And when we're home, she can come in again, the following Monday."

"And how are you going to get Bernard home, will he be fit to travel?"

"Oh, yes. He has a friend, a doctor here in London, who's looking after him. They were at Queen's together."

"Well, that's good. I mustn't keep you on the phone. Give Bernard our best regards and safe home."

"I will. Thanks, Agnes. Good night."

When she went back into the kitchen, Eileen was sitting at the table not eating her supper, just staring out the window. "What did she want to talk to you about?" Eileen asked.

"She said for me to make sure you took a week's extra holiday. Isn't that nice of them in the middle of their own troubles."

"Yes. Yes, it is."

"I made a treacle cake, could you manage a bit of it afterward?"

"Treacle cake," Eileen said. She gave a wan smile. "You went to a lot of trouble."

"Oh, it was no trouble. It passed the time. Tell me. I heard you talking about a machine to Mona, you were asking if he was off the machine yet? What sort of a machine is that?"

"Machine?" Eileen said. "I don't know what sort of a machine it was, it was just that she told me he was on some sort of machine."

Agnes Hughes decided that from the flustered way Eileen answered there was something more here than met the eye, but maybe it was better to ask no more questions. And when Eileen had eaten a bit of the treacle cake and they had had a cup of tea, she suggested that perhaps it would be a good idea for Eileen to go on up to bed. "Seeing you've had such a long day."

"I will. I'm dropping. But what about you, Mama, would you not like me to wait a while and help you undress?"

"No, no, I've been doing rightly on my own. It's good practice for me. You go on up. I'll be up later."

When Eileen went upstairs, her mother cleared away and went into the front sitting room. She turned on the telly, automatically, before she remembered there was no picture. After she had turned it off again, she sat for a good while thinking about Eileen's coming home early and being upset and Mona's phone call and the mysterious machine. And, of course, what she had been thinking about earlier this week, that report Eileen had given her on Monday about being left with Bernard while Mona went off on her own. There was something Eileen was not telling her. Still, there was no sense saying anything to her just now.

[194]

She went to bed around midnight. At two in the morning she heard sounds on the stairs and was afraid, was it a burglar? But then recognized Eileen's step. She heard her go into the kitchen below. Then heard her come upstairs again to her room. Eileen's bed was an old single bed that always squeaked when she got into it. There was no squeak. Agnes Hughes listened for a time, then got up quietly and went out on the landing. Eileen always slept with her door open, and now as her mother looked across the landing she saw a silhouette by Eileen's window, the girl sitting there looking out at the moonlit street. She stood watching her for a moment, then went over, her footsteps announcing her presence on the landing's floorboards. Eileen turned from the window and put on her bed light as her mother came in.

"All you all right, dear?"

Eileen nodded. "I just couldn't sleep. Go back to bed, Mama. Sorry to wake you."

"What's the matter, dear? There's something the matter, isn't there?"

"No, nothing, Mama."

"Give us a kiss, then."

They embraced. "Now, go back to bed, Mama. You're the one who needs your sleep."

"All right, dear. Good night."

When she was back in her own bed, she heard the creak of Eileen's bedsprings. And then, very quietly at first, she heard her daughter begin to sob. What had happened there, in London? It must be something more than just her holiday being spoiled. But she decided not to let Eileen know she had heard her crying. She knew that some griefs are best borne alone.

September

In the week that followed, Eileen did not go in to work in McAuleys shop. She seemed glad of the time on her own and went out a lot, always telling her mother that she was going for a walk. On Thursday she came back around three, made her mother a cup of tea, and announced that she had been looking for a new job and that she had a very good chance of becoming Dr. Davison's receptionist next month when his present receptionist was leaving to get married. She said that she wanted a change. She said no matter how good the pay and opportunities were, she had decided that she did not want to spend any more time working in a shop. She said that she would have liked to do nursing, but as that was not possible, she thought that being a doctor's receptionist was the next best thing. You were dealing with patients and forms for the Health Service and so on. Besides, Dr. Davison seemed very nice, he was young and new in practice and married with two young children. Agnes Hughes had met Dr. Davison once while her own doctor was on holiday. She said, yes, he seemed a nice sort of fellow and a good doctor. She did not say anything about how the McAuleys would take Eileen's leaving. Her daughter's mind seemed made up and, certainly, from the time she spoke about the new job she was a different girl. She lost the wan look she'd had since she came back from London.

Every night that week Mona McAuley rang up and talked to Eileen. It seemed Bernard was much better and they would both be coming home on Friday but would go on to Connemara the following week because Bernard needed to rest. On the Friday Mona and Bernard were due back, Agnes Hughes suggested it would be nice if Eileen went up to their house in Clanranald Avenue with flowers. But Eileen said she would ring Mona first. She did, and Mona said she would like to see her on Saturday afternoon, if that would be convenient. Agnes Hughes wondered if she should go too, but Eileen said, no, I want to tell Mona about this chance of a new job and I think it would be better if I did it alone. And no flowers.

And so on Saturday, a little after three, Eileen took the bus out of town, because Clanranald Avenue was about a mile out of Lismore on the Dublin Road. It was a long avenue of large Victorian houses, each set in its own grounds. The Mackies, who owned the Ulster Linen Works, lived in Clanranald Avenue, and the Unionist Member of Parliament for the district, Colonel Gough, had the corner house just off the Dublin Road. The McAuleys were the only Catholics in Clanranald Avenue. Their house was one up from Colonel Gough's and was one of the older and bigger houses in the avenue, with massive iron gates and the name TULLYMORE chiseled on its white stone gateposts. It was a wet afternoon, drizzling and dark, the sort of afternoon that would make the Garden of Eden look a misery, but when Eileen went through the gates into the driveway of Tullymore she was struck by the beautiful way the front grounds were kept up, the clipped hedges, the arrangements of rosebushes, the perfect lawn, and the clean white stones of the gravel drive on which her shoes made a crunching noise as she walked toward the house. She had been to this house only three times before, twice at parties and only once during the day, when Mona took her home to offer her the loan of a dress and coat for the trip to Dublin. It was the sort of house where the furniture was so good and the carpets so clean and the glassware so delicate that she was sure she would break something or spill something or have to deal with some point of etiquette she did not know about. Now, of course, there was Bernard to make her more nervous than before, for while she guessed he would not appear, she knew that he was here someplace and might even be watching her as she came up the drive. She saw a lattice fence running alongside the side of the house and, inside it, a big vegetable garden. She knew there was a flower garden at the rear of the house and, beyond it, double grass tennis courts. The house itself was three stories high, painted a cream color, with a big green front door ornamented with a brass bell and a brass knocker in the shape of a dolphin. It was a house that her mother said must take a lot of keeping up and the McAuleys had the services of a full-time gardener, a full-time maid, and, of course, Mrs. Kane, who was Mona's cook and housekeeper.

Now, as she came up to the front door and folded her umbrella under the cover of the porch, she saw someone move behind the bay windows of the front drawing room on her left. She rang and the door was opened almost at once by old Mary, who had been a maid in Bernard's father's house and was still in Bernard's service, although she was a bit past it. Mary wore an old-fashioned maid's uniform, black pinafore, white apron and cap, and as she reached for Eileen's wet umbrella, she bobbed in a sort of curtsy and said: "Good afternoon, miss, the mistress is expecting you." And when Eileen came into the hall after carefully wiping her feet on the doormat, there was Mona coming from the back of the house to embrace her. Mona wore a beige cashmere suit with beige kid shoes. Her hair was beautifully done and she looked serene and gracious in a way she did not look when you saw her outside her house. It was as though this house was her frame, a frame which set her off from other, more ordinary people.

"Eileen, how are you. Come on in, isn't that a desperate day?" Mona said, leading her toward the drawing room, ignoring old Mary, who followed along on faltering heels.

"Excuse me, ma'am, but would you like tea now?" old Mary wanted to know, but Mona did not look at her, saying: "I'll ring," and closing the drawing-room doors, shutting Mary out. Eileen went on into the room; it was the smaller drawing room, she knew. They had a bigger drawing room on the first floor, next to Bernard's study. But even this room was bigger than the whole ground floor of her mother's house in Church Street. There was a lamp lit in the room because the day was so dark, and light from it fell on chairs and sofas covered in cream-colored *bainin*, across a low table on which sat a big white ironstone vase filled with dark-red roses. A fire burned in the grate under an Adam chimneypiece. There were magazines on a green Connemara marble pier table and, everywhere, little silver dishes with sweets in them. Over the fireplace Eileen saw a large oil portrait of a man in the clothes of a former time, a man with an ugly but distinguished face. Was he some relative of Bernard's? But as she came closer she saw the little gold plaque on the frame: DANIEL O'CONNELL. THE LIBERATOR.

"Is that what he looked like?" she said, turning to Mona. "It's not like the pictures you see of him in the schoolbooks."

"It's supposed to be authentic," Mona said. "It was painted in his lifetime. Anyway, sit up to the fire. Would you ever believe this summer?"

Eileen sat in an armchair at the left of the fire. Mona took up a poker and knelt in front of the fire to poke the coals. Then, as though they were spies who had exchanged the password, they suddenly looked at each other.

"How is he?"

"He's all right. He'll be all right."

"You were worried about his memory, you said."

"No, he's all right now. But he's depressed. Oh, by the way, we're going to say it was hepatitis. Do you know what that is?"

"You get it from dirt in food, isn't it? Somebody going to the bathroom and not washing their hands?"

"That's right," Mona said. "And people are often depressed after it. They can be depressed for as long as a year or more, Derek said. So that's what we're going to say, in case people notice. It may take a bit of time, you know."

She looked up at Eileen as she said this, then replaced the poker on the firedogs and stood up, smoothing her skirt. "That's why I wanted to see you." She stood now with her back to the fire, looking down at Eileen. "We're going off to Connemara, as I told you. We'll be gone at least two weeks. I'm hoping he'll be a lot better by the time we get home again. Now, I was thinking. You know the City of Paris, don't you?"

"The dress shop?"

"Well, it's not generally known, but we have the controlling interest in that business."

"I thought it was a Belfast firm that owned it."

"They did. But Bernard bought them out. It's doing very well now, and, as a matter of fact, we're thinking of opening a shop with the same name and along the same lines in Dublin, probably next spring."

The City of Paris was the best dress shop in Lismore. Eileen had wandered in and out of it many's the time but thought the things too dear for her. Who would have guessed that the McAuleys owned it, too?

"I've been thinking," Mona said. "It's off on its own and we have no immediate connection with it, so Bernard never goes in there. What I'm proposing to you is that I arrange for you to go to work in the shop here to be trained as a manageress. And then, when we open the Dublin shop in the new year, if all goes well, we'll put you in as assistant manageress there. We could arrange to sell your mother's house here and get a nice wee flat for the pair of you in Dublin. And, in return, all you have to do is promise me you'll not see Bernard, even if he asks to see you. Which I don't think he will, but you never know. And don't go into our shop, or up King Street, Bernard's always in King Street now, with the builders. You know what I mean." She looked at Eileen, smiled, then put her hand on Eileen's shoulder. "It's a hard old road for all of us," she said. "But at least you'll not lose on this. That could be a great job for you in the City of Paris in Dublin, it's going to be just off Grafton Street, very central. You'd have a good salary and commissions. I'll draw up an agreement with you and give you guarantees."

"Does Bernard know about this?"

"Of course. We discussed it last night. He wants to help you. He wants to do what will be best for you. I mean, he knows that he was foolish and unrealistic and that speaking to you in the way he did left you no alternative. Anyway, I'll be honest with you, we need your cooperation and we're prepared to compensate you for it. And I'm sure that, in time, if we all behave sensibly, it will work out for the best. I'm hoping that, for Bernard, it will be a case of out of sight, out of mind. So . . . what do you say?"

As she listened to Mona, Eileen felt herself gripping the armrests of her chair as though tensing for a car collision. The McAuleys sitting down together once again to arrange other people's lives to suit them. A good job in Dublin, assistant manageress of a dress shop off Grafton Street, in return for her promise that she would hide herself from them forevermore. That was what it was, wasn't it? They would put a rope around her and stake her out someplace where she couldn't harm them. And now Mona was waiting, standing with her back to the fire, here in her beautiful house, wearing her expensive cashmere suit, smiling: a little anxious, but confident, waiting for her answer. Eileen looked up at Mona, and for the first moment ever in her dealings with the McAuleys, she was master. She was free.

"I suppose I've been thinking the same thing in a way," she said.

"Oh?" Mona smiled, puzzled.

"I mean that we'd better not see each other anymore. So I've got another job. I'm starting at the beginning of the month."

"What job?"

"With Dr. Davison. I'm going to be his receptionist."

"Receptionist?"

"Yes. So what I thought is, if it's suitable for you, I won't go back into the shop. You've given me the week off and I have some holiday time still due me. If I take that now, it will tide me over till I start with Dr. Davison in about three weeks. You could send my money and cards and all that by post to our house."

"When did you get this job?"

"A couple of days ago."

"But I was speaking to you on the telephone every day. Why didn't you tell me?"

"I thought you had enough to worry about without talking to me about jobs."

Mona was silent. For about half a minute all was quiet in that large, handsome room. Eileen heard the ticking of an ornamental clock. Then Mona sat in the armchair opposite her and said: "Well, that was very thoughtful of you, Eileen. I'm impressed. But actually, thinking it over, there's no need for you to lose on this. I mean, a receptionist's job wouldn't have the future the City of Paris would have. So think it over. In fact, I'd say you'd be foolish not to take my offer. Dublin would be great fun for you, and your mother's always saying she'd like to get out of Lismore. This hole!" And she laughed. "Bernard's right. We all know it's a hole, not that we dare say it out loud."

"I've told Dr. Davison that I'm starting with him. I'd prefer that."

"Why? Is it because you don't want to be beholden to us after what's happened? Is that it?"

"No, it's not. It's just—just that I don't want to go on working in shops. I've always wanted to do nursing and this might be the next best thing."

"I see." Mona frowned at her feet, as though she had noticed some imperfection in her perfect kid shoes. "Well, of course, it's your decision."

"Yes. I think it will be better this way."

"What does your mother say?" Mona asked. "You haven't told her what happened, have you?"

"No. She knows I wanted to do nursing. Don't worry about my mother. That's all settled."

As she said this, Eileen stood up. "Talking about my mother, I'd better get back home. I'm going to take her out to the shops this afternoon."

"Oh, but you'll have some tea. I'll just ring," Mona said, getting up and going to the wall where there was a bell push.

"No, thanks, really."

"Are you sure? Will I give you a lift back?"

"No, thanks."

"Well," Mona said. She did not seem to know what to say. She rang the bell, then went with Eileen to open the drawing-room doors. Old Mary came from the rear of the house. "Do you want tea now, Mrs. McAuley?"

"No, thanks, Mary. Miss Hughes is in a hurry. Do you have her umbrella?"

As old Mary bustled off to the closet, Mona said: "That's all right then, about the shop. Don't bother to come in. I'll send you your cards and three months' wages."

"I don't want three months' wages."

"Oh, come on," Mona said. "There's no need to be like that."

"I don't want it," Eileen said. "Please, don't sent it."

"Here's your umbrella, miss," Old Mary said, coming up. "It's still a bit damp, although I opened it to let the water run off. Still, the rain's over, by the looks of it."

"Thanks, Mary." She took the umbrella and Mary opened the front door. She turned to Mona. "Well, goodbye, then."

Mona forced her face into a smile. "I'll give you a ring when we get back from Connemara," she said.

Eileen shook her head no.

Mona smiled again, bravely, the smile of someone who turns the other cheek. "All right, whatever you say," she said very quietly, so that old Mary, behind her, did not hear. Eileen turned and went out the front door, looking up at the gray sky, which still threatened rain. She held her umbrella as though she would raise it, but as the front door closed behind her, she lowered the umbrella and began to walk very quickly, her shoes crunching on the gravel of the immaculate driveway as she went toward the heavy iron front gates. Behind her she felt the presence of the rich people's house, the presence of the McAuleys, knowing that Mona stood in the hall and that Bernard was somewhere upstairs, perhaps peering down at her this very minute; the McAuleys she had known and might never see again, the McAuleys who had had her in their power and who she now left behind in their big house as she hurried toward her freedom, the McAuleys who she had dismissed before they could dismiss her, who would try to go on as though nothing had happened, arranging things to suit themselves.

But as she shut the gates behind her and went out into Clanranald Avenue, her head full of these thoughts, it came to her, at last, that she was wrong. It was not she who had been in their power but they in hers. She had escaped them. Would they escape her?

Monday, November 20

In 1886, at a time of great prosperity in the linen trades, the mill owner who later became Lord Lismore presented his native town with a park. It was a small park set off on a hillside at the north end of Lismore, a wooded site in which he installed an artificial lake, floral gardens, a bowling lawn, and a bandstand for concerts which were given by British Army units from the nearby Connaught Barracks. In the nineteen-thirties, when the park had fallen into some disuse and was no longer popular as a Sunday strolling ground, the town council installed a concrete playground to replace the floral gardens, which had not been kept up. There were swings and a roundabout, a slide and a jungle gym.

Two months after Eileen went to work for Dr. Davison as his receptionist, Dr. Davison's wife came down with flu. The children had been cooped up in the house all weekend, as the Davisons had been unable to find a sitter, and so on Monday morning when Eileen came in to work, Dr. Davison told her to phone around and try to arrange for someone to come in and look after the children. She had no luck, and when the afternoon surgery was over, she volunteered to take the children out for a walk. Mrs. Davison said they liked the playground in Lismore Park and it didn't close until five, and although it was after four and would soon be dark at that time of year, Eileen put little Meg in the stroller, took Timmy, the older child, by the hand, and set off for Lismore Park.

She had not been in the park for ages. Nobody went there now except a few mothers to the playground and old men who played chess in the shelters and lovers to lie in the bushes when it was not wet and some boys to kick football between improvised goalposts made up of their piled jackets. From the Davisons' house you came to the park by a side gate, and so to get to the playground you had to go up the hill and over, passing through the wooded part, which was called the Ramble.

She was not very happy about that, especially not this late in the afternoon, for there were stories about men who hung out in the Ramble. A boy had been molested there last year, and there were cases of men exposing themselves to girls who walked through the park on a short cut to the Ulster Linen Works. So as Eileen went up the hill into the Ramble, pushing the stroller with Timmy dawdling behind her, she was not pleased to see a man coming toward her, a man wearing no hat and his raincoat collar up as if to hide his face.

She called to Timmy and made him take her hand. As she did, the man coming toward her seemed to hesitate, then came on more slowly. She saw why. It was Bernard McAuley. His face was puffy, and the first thing she thought was that he was getting fat, Bernard, who had always been a fanatic about his weight. His hair was wet and his overcoat was soaked through, as though he had been walking all afternoon in the rain. When he came level, he stopped, and smiled an uneasy smile. "Hello there."

"Hello."

"I never expected to run into you in this place," he said.

"No. Right enough." They stood, fidgeting their feet in the manner of people who have met and want to move on.

"Whose kids?"

"Dr. Davison's. I have to take them to the playground. We're late. It will be closing soon."

"Yes, I suppose so."

She bobbed her head in an awkward gesture of farewell. "I'll have to be going, then."

"Right." He went off down the hill. She gripped the stroller handles tight, pushing it forward. "Come on, Timmy. Hurry up." But Timmy was slow. She turned back to take his hand, and as she did she saw that Bernard had stopped farther down the path and was looking back at her. When he saw that she had seen him, he swiveled around and went off downhill in his swift, half-running stride.

"Who's that man?" Timmy asked.

"Never you mind. Come on!"

At the top of the hill, when she reached the playground railings, she again looked back down the path. There was no one there.

Thursday, December 30

Four days after Christmas some contractors who were to meet with Bernard McAuley at a building site rang his house when he did not show up. There was no answer. The following morning he was found dead in bed by his housekeeper. His wife was in Dublin at the time, arranging for the opening of a new dress shop. An autopsy determined that he had died of a mixture of sleeping pills and alcohol. His wife told the coroner that he had been in poor health and in low spirits ever since an attack of infectious hepatitis earlier that year.

The funeral was held in St. Patrick's Church, Lismore. Agnes Hughes attended, but her daughter did not. His wife was his sole legatee, and a few months later the house in Clanranald Avenue was put up for sale, as were all the shops and pubs and other businesses. When the estate was settled, Mona McAuley moved to London. People from the town who met her over there said she looked very well and was buying a big house in Chelsea. Eileen never saw her again.

Eileen Hughes, twenty years old and never before out of Northern Ireland, has just arrived in London for a week's holiday with Bernard and Mona McAuley, who are not only her employers but also, she believes, her great friends and benefactors. Bernard, at thirty-four, is the richest Catholic businessman in the town of Lismore, and his beautiful and sensual young wife has adopted Eileen as her special pet. Shy, virginal Eileen lives with her widowed mother, a semi-invalid; she looks on this trip as a truly great occasion.

This is the opening situation of Brian Moore's fourteenth book, and as one might expect from Ireland's greatest contemporary novelist, an intriguing story, beautifully told, grows out of it. The McAuleys are frequently—though subtly—at odds with each other, and Mona often disappears from their hotel, leaving Bernard to do the sightseeing and dining out and theatergoing with Eileen. Bernard, who is bright and amusing, turns out to be a man of strange romantic and religious beliefs. During the few days in which most of the novel's action takes place, Eileen discovers that nothing between the McAuleys, or between the